SEAWAYMEN

John Wingate

SAPERE
BOOKS

SEAWAYMEN

Published by Sapere Books.

20 Windermere Drive, Leeds, England, LS17 7UZ,
United Kingdom

saperebooks.com

ISBN: 978-1-80055-643-0

To Sukie and Rob on the other side of the world, is this book dedicated with my love and gratitude.

ACKNOWLEDGEMENTS

I should like to express my gratitude to those who have helped me in the preparation of this book. I wish to thank the Embassy of the Republic of Singapore, Paris; Mr Abdul Jabar, Press Officer of the Malaysian Foreign Affairs Department, Kuala Lumpur, for his friendship and good advice; Mr Herbert Teo, Public Relations Officer, Port of Singapore Authority, for his kindness, and Lieutenant A. R. C. Bell, Royal Navy, for his advice on the operation of helicopters.

In particular, my thanks are due to Captain A. C. Sprigings, Operations Manager, Cunard-Brocklebank, for his considerable contribution; and to Lieutenant-Commander R. B. Richardson, Royal Navy, (Ret'd), FRIN: without his professional guidance, enthusiasm and encouragement, this book could not have been written.

The characters in this record are fictitious, but if anyone should recognize themselves, the fact is coincidental and I offer my apologies.

— John Wingate, 30 July 1978

CHAPTER ONE

Azan Hamzah felt his age as he shuffled wearily forward along the schooner's deck. The planks beneath his leathery feet were already cooling in the evening breeze that was sighing across the silver surface of the sea. He reached the main boom, pushed against it and overhauled the sheets; the long pole creaked to leeward, the mainsail slatted across, and *Bunga Raya*, his forty-seven-year-old fishing schooner, filled as she leaned to the wind. Azan moved aft and took the helm; the channel was tortuous until the island of Pulau Selat Kering was well past his port quarter; not until *Bunga Raya* had cleared the south-easterly extremity of North Sands Bank, could he hand over to his son, Jaafar.

They had started fishing before dawn. From habit, Azan had taken his boat up to the Angsa Bank, the traditional fishing ground northwest of Port Swettenham, renamed since Independence, Pelabuhan Kelang. Since the tanker collision last year, the fish were disappearing from the bank, but there were still fishermen who worked their traps off the coast to the north of Selangor. One of these optimists was his brother and they had hailed each other across the water, while *Bunga Raya* had fished vainly the whole of the forenoon. The Hamzah fish-trap was one of the most southerly platforms, a V-shaped affair, with its apex stemming the flood stream. His brother, too, was growing old: he could not be bothered to renew the rickety platform, almost awash at high water, and held together by rotting, criss-crossed bamboos. Disillusioned by the decreasing fish, bewildered by the black menace creeping in on the tides from the sunken tanker, Azan Hamzah was succumbing to despair. The old man would be giving up when the southwest monsoon began in May…

Jaafar had shouted that they were wasting precious time up here on the Angsa Bank. Too dispirited to argue, Azan had agreed to try further south, to fish towards Port Dickson. The schooner had sailed down the North Kelang Strait during the afternoon, then slipped past the heavily wooded islet of Pulau Ketam that had been the home of the Hamzah family for centuries. The village and the red roof of the police station had slid swiftly past, as the boat swilled down on the flood — and now she was feeling the first of the swell as she cleared the narrows and dipped to the open sea — the old lady was alive again.

Azan was proud of his boat, one of the finest schooners surviving on the coast. If a boat looked right, she was usually an efficient fishing vessel if worked properly — and *Bunga Raya* (he had named her after the commonest of Malayan flowers) was one of the fastest of the Bugis schooners: with her white spars and masts, her sleek lines and her arrow-shaped prow for the spearman and lookout, she was part of the sea in which she toiled.

The old man shivered momentarily with the first chill of dusk, where he stood by the wheel in the square deckhouse abaft the mainmast. The sun was plummeting below the horizon, and already the lowering night clouds were streaked blood-red to the westward. By mid-morning the usual sea breeze had got up, freshening to strong during the afternoon — Force 6 when it combined with the southwest monsoon. But now, when they most needed it, the breeze was dying away. Azan would set a course of 175° for the three-metre patch on South Sands Bank, which used to be one of the best areas. He would start the engine: at her seven knots, *Bunga Raya* should be fishing again by 2030. His son, Jaafar, had slept long enough. The pounding of the diesel would rouse him from his bunk; he could take the schooner across the shipping lanes while the nets were flaked.

The old man felt a tap on his shoulder. Jaafar was a good son and Azan twitched a toothless grin at the bearded young man who was already twenty-two.

'The land breeze might get up before we reach mid-channel,' Azan murmured. 'Watch out for the shipping.'

From the corners of his wrinkled eyes, he watched his youngest son: the boy had been trained from childhood to take over the fishing when the time was right. Azan had brought him up severely, knowing that the sea was a hard mistress — and Jaafar had spent his youth amongst boats and fishermen. Coastal seine-netting, fish traps with their offshore bamboo platforms, push-nets, line-fishing and drift-netting from the elegant *praus* in the estuaries — Jaafar had worked them all.

To the Malay people, fishing was in the blood — Azan's countrymen lived on rice and on the fish that once filled the warm waters washing Malaysia's long coastline. The life had been hard for Jaafar. The market began at dawn, the fish glistening in profusion on the stalls. The heat of the midday sun soon spoiled the catch, and it paid to be early with the landing. Though each year that passed brought fewer and fewer fish, at least the price was going up — a factor which was worrying the politicians. The price of fish had rocketed: the carp, squid, cuttlefish, crabs and cockles were twice as dear as they had been ten years ago. But the Malay favourite, the heaps of *ikan bilis*, minute sprats, were becoming more and more difficult to gather. Azan was convinced that the breeding grounds had become infected by the last tanker's pollution.

'I'm steering 175°, Jaafar. A couple of ships are coming up from the southeast — see their lights?'

'Yes, Father. I've got her: I'll call you when we're off South Sands.'

Jaafar's outline filled the deckhouse window. Though too sensitive, he was a fine man now, nearly two metres tall and a Pulau Ketam islander from birth. They had been forced to lay off another deckhand, and Jaafar's strength was essential for the working of the schooner. But he had recently become morose and detached — the worries of his young family, Azan supposed. His wife was a good woman, but their third child had increased their financial problems, for even with today's government help, mouths were becoming increasingly difficult to feed. The fishing was dying — and Azan moved silently below, nursing his depression. He had no one with whom to discuss things now: he had been a widower for too long and he was tired, very tired.

The slatting of the sails was fraying Jaafar's nerves. He called the deckhand to brail up the loose-footed mainsail. He watched the seaman shinning up the ratlines, checked that the sail was properly furled, then settled down to his watch, the coughing of the diesel exhaust a background to the hiss of the sea along the waterline.

The night was dark, the sea ebony in this glassy calm. The tanker in ballast had slipped past, another Japanese vessel, he supposed, on passage to the Gulf for more oil. Only her navigation and a few accommodation lights gleamed in the darkness: the phosphorescence of her wake sparkled astern of her, a diminishing trail to the hazy horizon. The other ship, a square box of a thing (probably one of those roll-on, roll-off ships) had passed clear astern; *Bunga Raya* was now on her own and crossing to the far side of the channel. The low-lying coast of Sumatra, over which the monsoon fanned, was invisible twenty miles to the southward.

He knew these waters as a farmer would know his fields — and yet Jaafar always sensed the flutter in his guts when he saw the phosphorescent trails of the water snakes. These reptiles abounded in the Malacca Strait, criss-crossing the surface on a calm night: he could distinguish them from the harmless varieties by their flat tails. Jaafar detested the sinister, highly poisonous creatures as much as the sailors feared the crocodiles which were encountered sometimes as far as thirty miles from the coast.

It was pitch-black over Sumatra. Lightning flashes sizzled along the horizon, but there was no rumble of thunder. If the boat had not been making way, the humidity would have been unbearable. The night was airless, hot and sticky, a sure indication that the usual blow was on its way. He glanced to the westward, searching for the typical line squall heralding an advancing 'Sumatra', as the storms were known locally. Within seconds, the sea would be whipped up by these howling squalls striking savagely from nowhere. When a rainsquall coincided with a Sumatra, a screaming fury sometimes reaching Force 10, the gusts could heel the schooner in seconds, the seas breaking white, a fearsome, foaming cauldron. A fishing boat caught on Malaysia's lee shore stood little chance, if she had not clawed off in time to gain sea room.

Luckily it was calm tonight … and then Jaafar saw the slick of oily water dead ahead.

The schooner was crossing a lane of filthy scum. He glanced over his shoulder to the northwest, then to port, to the southeast. The spattered lane led into the darkness, stretching for miles. Some rogue tanker was washing tanks, a forbidden operation nowadays. He had once followed the wash of an unidentified tanker who had been surreptitiously washing her tanks for four hours. Forbidden the practice might be, but who could identify the culprit in low visibility? Who could prosecute? And who could punish, when the ship was, officially, on the High Seas?

Jaafar felt bitter. The continuous erosive effect of oil pollution, a few more tons each week, was having its remorseless effect on the Malay Peninsula's beautiful coasts and beaches. The first to suffer the effects were, as usual, the fishermen. He and all the village were behind the government when it declared a twelve-mile limit, in support of Indonesia's decision to do the same. Yet the superpowers were insisting that the Straits should remain international waters; and neither did Japan like Indonesia's decision. Already, Japan was having too much say in the matter by insisting on producing her own survey. And now she was threatening to escort her own ships to protect them from international action by the coastal nations.

The fact that the Malay Peninsula and Indonesia could now close the Strait if they wished was causing much agitation in the international courts on the Law of the Sea. But while the lawyers argued, the fishing industries and the marine ecology of Malaysia, Singapore and Indonesia were suffering remorseless, certain deaths. Emotions were easily aroused, and each trip that ended with poor catches added fuel to the discontent.

The schooner slid from the fouled water, and into the black mirror-surface once again. Jaafar flicked the knob of the echo sounder — 25 metres... She must be across the lanes and approaching South Sands, a bank which shelved rapidly ... 21 ... 18, shallowing to the 10-metre line... He spun the wheel, bringing her to port: he would follow the line of the bank which formed the southerly limit to the Deep Water Route. He knocked back the throttle and nodded to the seaman on deck.

'Shake the hands — let the old man sleep.'

As the schooner lost way, he felt the gentle breeze across the starboard gunwale. He would set the jibs and mainsail, then slide down on the tide, while they shot the drift nets.

The for'd lookout had just reported the black and white buoy, right ahead and flashing every five seconds. The soundings were increasing: *Bunga Raya* must be ahead of her Dead Reckoning position. The clock showed four o'clock and it was time for Jaafar to change the watches. He would bring her round: pick up the white sector of Kuala Sepang Besar light, then set course for the confused waters off Bambek shoal, six miles west of Port Dickson. Twilight was at 0543 and they could try their luck all day off these banks — it was pointless to enter the harbour as planned: the catch was not worth landing. The old man, who had come up for Pyramid shoal, had returned in disgust to his pit...

'Course, 035°,' the helmsman reported, as one of the hands hailed from aft.

'Ship coming up on our port quarter, master...'

Jaafar turned. A green light and the steaming lights of a ship were bearing down upon them. She loomed from the dawn haze, which usually formed when the humidity was high. She was less than a mile off and was steering northwards, between Pyramid shoal and the southern extremity of South Sands.

'She's outward from Dumai,' he shouted. 'She's well down to her marks.'

A coastal tanker of about 4,000 tons, she was probably one of the shuttle service between the Caltex refinery at Dumai, behind the low-lying island of Rupat, and the terminals dotted along the Malay Peninsula's western shore. If she turned to the east, she would discharge at Esso's terminal jetty off Point Kamuning, though the smaller tankers discharged at Shell's jetty to the west of Railway Jetty. At the entrance to Port Dickson, the new facilities, with their floating oil-hoses and underwater pipelines, were a nuisance these crowded days. With the port's huge generating station and its tall chimney painted with red, white and black bands; with the two refinery flares flickering from their booms, Port Dickson was not difficult to identify from seaward...

Jaafar kept *Bunga Raya* steady on her course, allowing the tanker to slip swiftly up her port side: he could just read her name — *Sulu*. When she was broad on the schooner's bow, he sighted for the first time the bow lights of a large ship emerging from the gloom to the northward. Her great bow lunged from the darkness, a bone in its teeth.

The east-bound ship was well over on her starboard side of the south-easterly lane, less than a quarter of a mile, Jaafar judged, from the twelve-metre shoal where the surface boiled in confused seas. Obviously restricted by lack of water, one long, then two short blasts boomed in the night from her siren.

Jaafar felt the presence of his father. The old man was peering through the night, mesmerized by the impending disaster: the features of his wizened face were working as he cursed silently to himself.

It was difficult to judge whether the VLCC (Very Large Crude Carrier) had begun swinging to port before her siren boomed again: four shorts, this time, an interval, then two more — an emergency turn to *port*, because she was the give-way ship. *Sulu* had held to her course, but she could have used more imagination and turned in plenty of time to starboard, to give manoeuvring room to the VLCC — *Sulu*'s master might have been more prudent and allowed for the possibility of the oncoming ship being a fully laden 'big boy'. Perhaps he was one of those idiots who enjoyed playing 'chicken', seeing whose nerve could hold for longer: crazy enough on the open seas on approaching courses, but suicidal in restricted waters — Jaafar had heard of such irresponsible captains. If he had his way, he would string them up to the nearest derrick…

Sulu was still holding on. Even if she … and then Jaafar heard her hooting four shorts, a pause, then another short. She was taking the only action possible now, apart from going full speed astern — and even that would be too late. He could not tear away his eyes.

His father was swearing foully and calling alternately upon the Prophet, as he gripped the coaming along the deckhouse with his scrawny hands. *Sulu* was swinging rapidly, her silhouette now aligned with the monstrous black ship, whose green light was just obscuring — and whose stern light was beginning to show. Their bows might clear, but there was a quarter of a mile of VLGG swinging outwards, to starboard, towards *Sulu*'s turning circle…

Jaafar heard the shattering noise of the collision, though the two tankers were more than a mile away: the screech of rending steel carried clearly across the water. A shower of sparks shot into the night sky, as *Sulu*'s counter sliced along the VLCC's starboard quarter. An orange flame flashed in the darkness. A steely-blue streak blinded him — then the blast of an explosion rattled the panes in the schooner's deckhouse.

'Look, Father — the big one's out of control.'

The old man hissed through his compressed lips and grabbed his son's arm. 'See,' he whispered. 'She'll be up on the bank any second.'

They watched in horror as *Sulu* flared into a glowing torch. The flames had flickered from somewhere aft, then danced along her length until she was a blazing inferno.

'Furl all sail,' Jaafar yelled to the hands huddled along the port side. 'We'll see what we can do.' As the men dispersed to their stations, the VLCC, turning under full port rudder, stopped suddenly, her bows heaving upwards.

'She's hard on... They'll never get her off,' the old man muttered. 'See, Jaafar, she'll be in that confused water, right amongst the tide rips...'

The whole north-western horizon seemed on fire, night being turned into day. *Bunga Raya* nosed ahead on her diesel. Already the Maydays were going out, the radio in the schooner's deckhouse crackling with distress calls to the lighthouse at Pelabuhan Kelang.

'*Mayday, Mayday, Mayday...* Delta Echo...' Jaafar heard the clipped speech of the operator who was using the international code. 'Delta Echo... *Iro Maru, Iro Maru, Iro Maru...* My position is 273°, Pulau Arang 24 miles. Aground on bank in broken water. Ship holed, believed in engine room and after cargo tanks. In collision with unknown medium tanker, name unknown, who is on fire. Immediate assistance required. *Mayday, Mayday, Mayday...*'

'Well, boy, what are you going to do?' The old fisherman was glaring at his son. There was a wildness in his eyes that Jaafar had never seen before.

'We'll stand by *Sulu*, Father,' he shouted. 'They'll be jumping into the water at any second.'

'Look after *Raya*, first,' the old man yelled angrily. 'Let the bastards burn.' He spat bitterly over the side.

Jaafar threw the gear lever into ahead. He felt the jolt as the schooner lurched towards the inferno.

CHAPTER TWO

Tim Simkins cursed and flicked into neutral for his red mini to coast up to the next car's bumper. The street ahead was blocked for as far as he could see and in his rear mirror, he watched the other early birds closing up behind. What was happening up front? On the one day he had decided to use the car, there had been a foul-up…

He had rolled out of bed at five-thirty, determined to start in the cool of the morning for his office. London Shipping was an easy-going outfit, allowing Tim a free hand, provided he produced results. Today he would try to get away in good time from the office, for he was meeting Cherry in the lunch hour, an interlude that was all too short. The bars were steamy at midday, and Cherry hated being kept waiting. Tim twisted the rear mirror to check his appearance, for she was fussy about the way he looked.

The face staring back at him was, he supposed, very ordinary. Cherry was trying to persuade him to shave off his beard: a magnificent growth, copper-tinged at the edges with swashbuckling mustachios. Tim smirked, those amused blue eyes acknowledging that it was a vanity to compensate for his height — he was just five foot eight, if he held himself upright. He had a barrel of a chest and he knew that he rolled rather than walked, even when in a hurry: these past years in modern, comfortable ships, and now his recent job, had made him overweight. His face wasn't bad — it was just that his head seemed too big for his body.

The van behind the mini was tooting impatiently. Tim slipped into first and the slow crawl into the city continued. He would be lucky to be in his office by eight-thirty.

The cause of the traffic chaos became clear when he reached the city centre: the police were trying to control a bunch of demonstrators who had effectively blocked the streets. Their banners, in spite of police charges, rocked back and forth above the surging crowd: 'CLEAN SEAS' and 'CLOSE THE STRAITS' vied with 'PROTECT OUR FISHERMEN' and 'HALT THE OIL BARONS'. Halted by the traffic jam, Tim strolled from his mini and bought a *Straits Times*. He had been out of touch with affairs during this last week: late nights at the office working on the company's latest sheep-ship conversion and his involvement with Cherry had divorced him from the outside world.

The front page was devoted entirely to the latest tanker incident in the Malacca Strait. A Japanese VLCC had collided with one of the Dumai inter-port carriers. The resulting explosions and spillage were disastrous to the Kelang and Port Dickson coast. These calamities were almost regular events now: hardly surprising with the density of traffic through the Straits and the disagreement between the three coastal nations over traffic control and the buoyage system. Then Tim's eyes caught a footnote, one of the tragedies that this oil problem was engendering more and more frequently, tucked away at the bottom of the right-hand corner:

The findings of the inquest on the death of Mr Azan Hamzah were announced today in Pelabuhan Kelang. The coroner found that Mr Hamzah, aged 72, took his life while the balance of his mind was disturbed. Mr Hamzah's body was found by fishermen on the high watermark at the entrance to the Buloh River. The deceased's son, Mr

Jaafar Hamzah, said that his father had been depressed recently over the decline in fishing due to the ravages of pollution in the Strait. Mr Jaafar Hamzah was skipper of the schooner, Bunga Raya, *who went to the assistance of the two tankers recently involved in the collision off Port Dickson. The late Mr Hamzah came from Pulau Ketam, a declining fishing village off Pelabuhan Kelang. He leaves two sons and a daughter; Jaafar Hamzah stated that he was thinking of selling the family schooner,* Bunga Raya.

Tim flung the paper onto the passenger seat, as the traffic jogged onwards again. The police were arresting some of the younger protesters and the road was clearing. The waterfront was sliding past as the road wound around the Boat Quay where the small craft lay, the motorized Chinese junks, the lighters and the old sampans. He caught sight of a painted notice fixed to the mast of one of the more gaily painted sampans: *For Sale.*

Tim had travelled a short distance before the idea came to him — this could be the solution to his and Cherry's accommodation problem. They could find a quiet corner and live in the sampan after they had tarted it up. Cherry was that sort of woman; she would enjoy a bit of pioneering — or would she? Brides these days expected modern kitchens and all mod-cons — but there was no harm in having a look, though he had no idea of today's values nor what it would cost to do the sampan up. He eased the car from the traffic and drove towards the quay. He might get away with parking for ten minutes at this peak hour...

Tim stood on the quayside, looking down at the old sampan: he could see her name, *Star of Heaven,* but there was no port of registry across her stern. And the more he looked at her, the more his imagination caught fire — he was falling in love with her already. He crossed the plank and tapped on the deckhouse door. No answer. He knocked loudly, waited, then tried the brass handle. Disappointed, he began walking back to his car. He turned for a last look: the door was half-open and a European head was visible through the crack. Tim hurried back across her sagging plank.

'Was it you knocking?' an American accent drawled.

'I saw your notice. I'm looking for a boat.'

'Come aboard. Pleased to show you around. My name's Harvey — Jake Harvey.'

'I'm Tim Simkins. I'm not too early, I hope?'

'No, sir! Come aboard.' The door opened and the bare chest of a broad-shouldered man appeared. He was grey-faced, unshaven, and his hair was tousled and greasy. A large wart, from which a tuft of hair sprouted, disfigured his left cheek. He was smiling dolefully and his eyes were suspicious — no way could Tim win with this character. The dark head disappeared below, into the gloom of the saloon. Tim crossed the plank and entered the deckhouse which was ornately and brightly decorated. The American was looking at him from below, sardonic amusement in his half-closed eyes.

'Yeah — I kept the joss element: I'm superstitious. Reckon you need it in these harbours...' He jerked his head towards the boat's side. Through the square port, the knobbly rubbing strake of what was once a stores lighter nudged *Star of Heaven*'s side. 'It's as crowded on the water as it is ashore these days. Come on down, sir.'

Tim's first impression was of ample space in the saloon — this beamy boat, built for river and estuary work, would make an ideal houseboat — he was surprised that some enterprising businessman had not taken up the idea. A large table stood amidships, a wicker affair with bamboo legs. In one corner was an old-fashioned heating stove; along the boat's sides stretched rows of shelves and cupboards.

'Would you care to see the rest? I'll start for'd.'

As Tim followed the hunched figure in blue jeans, a second impression struck him: the scent of burnt joss sticks pervaded the old sampan. A sensual, aromatic perfume lingered on the air. He followed the owner through a curtained partition and into a passage; the American was holding open a door on the port side.

'I did this myself...' He was smiling whimsically, as he pointed to a compartment covered with blue and purple tiles. 'Had to have a shower and heads,' he was saying. 'Yes, it flushes — salt water.' He laughed as he added, 'Doreen insisted on all mod-cons. I'll lead the way, sir. She'll be glad to make your acquaintance.'

Tim hesitated, then followed into the bedroom, a broad compartment in the forepart, the enclosed forepeak forming the limiting bulkhead. A woman stood facing him, buttoning up her floral housecoat, a comb in her hand as she continued putting up her hair.

'Sorry to bother you so early,' Tim said. 'But I'm on my way to the office; I saw your boat was for sale.'

She drew the comb through her black tresses. 'Feel free,' she said. 'It's Jake's idea to sell.' Her head jerked to the rumpled bed taking up the length of the starboard side. 'Haven't had time to tidy up...'

The disorder and the general air of lassitude were depressing, but Tim was sure he and Cherry could soon transform this shambles. Together they could make a home of this, as long as the hull was sound.

'Thanks,' Tim said. 'May I see the engine?'

Harvey led the way aft, through the saloon, up to the deckhouse, then down to the cramped, enclosed box containing the diesel with its massive fly-wheel.

'She's a beaut,' the American said. 'Never let me down yet.' He flicked the decompression stops and pressed the starter. The engine groaned, then pumped into life. 'Brought us safely down from Bangkok,' he said. 'No trouble.'

'Ever had the boat surveyed?' Tim asked.

The American's face shut tightly, like a blind being drawn across a window. 'Surveyed? I don't…'

'How old is she?' Tim asked.

'They told me she was forty years old when I bought her. She's teak throughout: sound as a bell. Not a drop of water…'

Tim was watching him, waiting for the crunch. He could halve the asking-price and still be the loser with this character. 'What price are you asking?'

'Twenty grand.' The American was peering through the port at the boats smothering the inner harbour like water beetles.

'Twenty thousand dollars?' Tim repeated incredulously.

'That's what she's worth.'

'I'm interested, but I'd want a survey.' Tim caught the flicker in the man's pale blue eyes.

'You want to see her bottom?'

'I'd insist on it.' There was a momentary silence, but before the American could reply, Tim added, 'I'll give you ten without the survey.' Even if they lived in her for a few years and they sold for half that figure, they could not lose, as long as she remained afloat. He sensed the woman standing behind him.

'Cash?' the American asked.

'Cash, but a bill of sale properly exchanged between us, signed at my solicitor's, providing my girlfriend likes her. We're getting married shortly, and this could be our home.'

The man hesitated. He glanced at the woman, then turned suddenly. 'Okay. She's yours, providing the sale's through pronto.'

'How quickly?'

'Can you do tomorrow?'

Tim laughed shortly. 'Pushing it, aren't you? She's not even registered.'

'Up to you. Those are my conditions at that price. You can register her yourself in Singapore.'

'I'll think about it and let you know on my way home this evening. Thanks for showing me round.'

'Bring your lady round — any time.'

'Tomorrow? About six?'

'Fine. See you then.'

Tim clambered out through the pagoda-like deckhouse, then picked his way across the plank to the shore. An old woman came up to him, shoving flowers in his face. He bought a bunch of orange *canna* for Cherry, then strolled towards his car. He was boxed in by a white Mercedes and Tim was sweating by the time he had extricated himself. He had kept his temper, but glared at the driver, a middle-aged man with a Zapata moustache, who grinned back. Tim drew away, then in his mirror he watched the Mercedes pull out. As the white saloon followed, he could still see the old flower woman waving a fistful of scarlet lilies. They looked like blood against the white walls of the shed behind her.

'What did you really think of it, Timothy?'

Cherry Hok lay stretched out on the settee which they had moved out onto the balcony of her eleventh-floor flat. She settled her head into his lap, stretching her slim fingers to his neck. They had come straight home from their offices and the smell of the curry she had prepared was making him hungry. Tim leaned back and stretched his legs against the balustrading. This was a delicious interlude in their new life, an oasis after a sweltering day of city routine, while they watched the sun galloping towards the horizon and the islands. Out there, ships were plying through the narrow channels, carrying their loads of crude eastwards to Japan, returning westwards in ballast to fetch further cargoes from the Persian Gulf — strings of them, one after another...

'Uh?'

'What did you really think of it, our *Star of Heaven*?'

'"Her", Cherry. To the mercantile English, ships are female.'

'You said it was a boat.'

'Boats are female too.' He leant forwards to kiss her. Her arms locked behind his neck. 'I want you, Cherry,' he said.

'When we're married,' she whispered. 'Wait until we're married. *Star of Heaven* can be our home. I don't have to see her first — *you* know all about boats. Oh, Tim, hurry and buy her.' Cherry pulled herself from his grasp and stood over him in the twilight, silhouetted against the deepening purple of dusk. 'I want you just as much as you want me,' she whispered, her fingers tracing the outline of his lips. 'But you know I want God's blessing on our union first...'

She left him and went inside. The candles she had lit flickered in the living room, and Tim could hear her singing in the kitchen. He stayed on the balcony. He had heard it all before: these converts to Christianity disliked bending the rules.

'I'll buy her tomorrow, then,' he shouted to her. 'She's a bargain at his lower price.'

'You'll fix it properly — through a solicitor?'

'Of course. I'll go to the bank early. His terms are cash.'

He heard the clatter of dishes as she laid the table. 'Why don't you come to *Star of Heaven* after the office tomorrow?' he called. 'I'll show you round properly. I'll ring you at your office when I'm ready.'

'I'll be late tomorrow. A terrible day... I'll wait for your call.'

'Then we'll get married?' Tim said, rising from the settee. Until he'd met Cherry, he'd never been the marrying sort.

'As soon as my parents can arrange it,' she called. He heard her pattering towards him across the rush matting of the living room. She flung herself into his arms, burying her head in his chest. 'I'm so happy,' she whispered.

Timothy Simkins sighed as he settled back in the seat of the Singapore bus. He hoped he would never experience another day like this: London had been on to him first thing, pressing him to hasten the sheep-pen conversions in *Baitulla*, formerly *London Reach*, which the company were preparing for the expanding live-sheep trade to the Gulf. The Singapore yard was first class, but could not produce miracles: there was much to be done to the fresh-water lines and to the drainage before the sheep accommodation could be started. He had hung up on London, when the bank manager rang to say that the arrangements for buying the sampan had been made. He had been surprised at Tim's request for cash — but had made no further enquiries.

When Tim finally walked into the bank on the waterfront, he had noticed a white Mercedes parked further down the road. Its two Malay occupants were staring across the harbour complex. Tim recognized one of them as the driver he had seen yesterday opposite the sampan — he was wearing the same garish shirt, with the words 'World Yacht Race' emblazoned across the chest. Tim had thought no more about it, until, looking through the rear window of the bus, he had noticed the Mercedes ease from the kerbside, after the bus had forged into the city traffic. The white car remained behind several vehicles and made no attempt to overtake.

The meeting with the American in the solicitor's office had been unremarkable, save that the lawyer seemed dismayed by Tim's haste. The American had signed, pocketed the cash and left as smartly as was decent.

'See you this evening, Mr Simkins? Okay? I'll keep my keys until then?'

'Yes, I've got my set. See you about seven.'

That had been before lunch, but after Tim's afternoon call on the shipping agent, the visit to the yard and the final clearing up in his office at the end of the day, he was feeling clapped out as he sat in the bus on his way to the boat quay. Tim loved Singapore, a relatively law-abiding city. Its new prime minister, the successor chosen by the republic's founder, Lee Kuan Yew, had continued with Yew's forceful policy of trying to eliminate the underworld. It had been a tough job, the heroin industry being what it was. The protectionism of the secret societies had been almost eliminated, but drug scandals still troubled the republic and its city. One of the focal points for world trade, Singapore engendered a bustling commerce, but the undeniable advantages also brought their evils.

The bus was drawing up to the last batch of lights before the boat quay. Tim always enjoyed this stretch, where the ancient traditions of the seafaring community rubbed shoulders with the civilization of the modern world. Office towers and accommodation blocks dwarfed the hundreds of small craft huddled in the port below. The smell of fish, tar and paint mingled with the exhausts of the traffic, in spite of the clean-air policy which the authorities enforced.

The bus lurched forward, then drew up by the quay. Tim jumped out next to the old flower woman. She grinned at him, thrusting another bunch of *canna* at him, a sheaf of bleeding crimson… *Star of Heaven* was further out, some lighter having wedged itself between her and the wall. He glanced over his shoulder, where a white Mercedes was drawing into the kerb further along the quay, its indicator blinking in the gathering dusk.

Tim had to cross two lighters before he reached *Star of Heaven*. There was a smell of cooking wafting on the evening air, but though it was almost dark, there was no welcoming glow from the saloon below, as from the other craft. All about him were the sounds of discordant music, soft conversation and the cries of children.

He tapped on the deckhouse door. He waited, knocked again.

'Mr Harvey?' Tim called down to the saloon, the door of which was shut. He descended the ladder. He stood motionless for a moment, listening outside the door, and called again, softly: 'Harvey?'

Tim's heart was thumping against his ribs as he carefully turned the handle. He leaned gently and the door creaked open. He fumbled for his lighter as he stepped into the dark saloon.

CHAPTER THREE

The lighter flame flickered, snuffed out. The cries of children and the cackling of fowls filtered through the open skylight above the saloon. In spite of the draught, there was an objectionable, musty smell about the boat, the same clinging odour that Tim had noticed yesterday.

'Mr Harvey...?'

He stumbled through the darkness, flicking his lighter as he ran the palm of his hand along the bulkhead for the light switch. A dim red light snapped on in the deckhead: there was still juice in her batteries...

'Harvey...' Tim called again, uncertain whether to proceed further, though *Star of Heaven* now belonged legally to him. Where was the Yank and his woman? He had said this evening, hadn't he? If both companionway doors were opened, more light would filter down from the lights outside. Tim turned back.

Curious: the door must have snapped shut without his noticing. He turned the handle. He pulled gently, but could not shift the door — jammed, probably. He would have a good look round — Harvey could not object and would be along soon. Tim spotted another switch and the boat's full lighting came on, a baleful gleam, probably from a twelve-volt supply. He decided to start methodically, beginning forward and working aft. He moved into the fore-cabin.

The compartment was in a shambles. The personal gear had gone, the centre table lay on its side, three of its legs smashed. The bunk was tipped up and someone had ripped the mattress open — the stuffing spilled across the rush-matting on the deck. A cupboard door hung from one hinge and all the other lockers were open, the shelves in savage disarray. A lamp bracket hung from the for'd panel, the bulb flickering in its disjointed connection.

'What the…?' Tim was muttering to himself, when he spotted a dark stain on the matting at the entrance to the cabin. He crouched and touched the rushes with his fingers. He felt the stickiness and recoiled in revulsion. He backed away from the cabin and moved into the saloon, holding his hands before him. He couldn't get to the basin quickly enough to wash off the blood. This was his boat — what had he let himself in for? He pushed aft the sliding door of the heads, heard it trundling along its tracks. He fumbled with his left hand for the light switch, blinked from the brightness of the neon and the gleaming tiles. He turned towards the basin. He froze, the hairs at the nape of his neck prickling at the horror confronting him…

Stuffed into the lavatory pan was a severed head. The eyes were staring upwards, fixed in death, terror still lurking in the depths of the irises. The parchment flesh was grey and the mole on the American's cheek still sprouted its stubble. His matted hair hung grotesquely across one side of his face, and a dribble of blood had coagulated at the corners of his blue lips…

As Tim backed slowly through the door, the nausea rose in his gorge. He jerked forwards and retched into the basin. He wiped the sweat from his forehead, wrenched at the collar of his shirt. As he glimpsed his white face in the mirror, he caught sight of the message scrawled in lipstick across the tiles above the cupboard:

EXECUTED FOR TREACHERY
KEEP OFF, SIMKINS
RED DRAGONS.

Tim floundered backwards from the heads. He slammed shut the sliding door. He subsided onto the leather seat surrounding the L-shaped bay of the saloon, his legs still trembling from the shock. Though he had spent fifteen years in the Merchant Service, he had not yet experienced the sight of death — but even for the most hardened of men this horror would have been too much. His only urge was to escape, to prevent Cherry from coming down to the sampan. Still mesmerized by the grisly image behind the door of the heads, he jerked to his feet and made towards the door to the companionway. He was again trying the handle when a voice from the skylight called stridently above him: 'Not so fast, Mr Simkins, we haven't finished with you yet.'

Tim paused, his shoulder against the door panel: that accent was certainly not Singaporean Chinese... At that instant, the door flew open, and four thugs burst into the compartment. Tim fell back as they padded in silence towards him, the blades of flick-knives glinting in their hands.

'What d'you want with me?' Tim gasped. 'I never knew the American.'

They were slowly encircling him. He retreated towards the corner of the settee, his back to the cupboards. He snatched at a brass rod used to stop the books slipping off the shelves. He spread his feet apart and faced them, the rod whistling as he flailed the air.

'I'll bash the brains out of the first one to move,' he yelled to the invisible man above. 'Tell 'em that.'

The man above said something and the thugs moved back a pace. Two of them began uncoiling a rope they had brought.

'We're leaving you to cool off,' their boss shouted down from the skylight. 'Resist, Simkins, and we'll slit your throat.'

Tim hesitated: it was useless to take on this bunch of killers. He had to play for time. 'Okay,' he called. 'What d'you want?'

'Answer my questions. Don't get excited or you'll join Harvey.'

Tim tossed the brass rod onto the settee. No use yelling — the racket outside would drown his cries. The thin chord bit into his wrists as they bound him and shoved him backwards onto the settee. They secured the ends of the rope tightly above his head, through the grille of the cupboard panelling. They stood back, grinning, then left the saloon. The door latch turned on the outside. He heard them talking softly with the man above the skylight.

'Who are you?' Tim yelled, trying to suppress the panic mounting inside him. 'Part of the Red Dragon set-up?'

'Don't shout,' the man murmured from above. 'If you call for help, I'll put a bullet through you.'

Tim could make out the rectangular patch of light above him, reflected from the lighting of the adjacent boats, but the invisible hatchet man was hidden behind the skylight on the port side. 'Why did you murder Harvey?' he shouted again. 'Why did he want to sell *Star of Heaven*?'

'That's what I want to know. Why has he sold the boat to you, Mr Simkins? And where's the cash you handed him? You did give him the money, didn't you, Mr Simkins?'

'Of course I did, in the solicitor's office.'

'Did Harvey talk to you?'

'What about?'

There was no immediate answer. Then the voice continued softly through the skylight: 'Don't play the innocent, Mr Simkins. And your woman, Cherry Hok — did he talk to her?'

'No. For God's sake, what are you driving at, you murderous bastard?'

'She's coming down to the boat for you?'

Tim hesitated momentarily. 'No, she's not. Let me go, you fool. I've no idea what all this is about — only that you've butchered the previous owner of this sampan.'

'When you don't return, she'll be down for you...'

'No,' he shouted. 'She's not expecting me tonight.'

The man chuckled softly. 'We'll wait to find out for ourselves. I've all the time...'

'Leave Cherry out of this,' Tim yelled angrily. 'She knows nothing — no more than I do. Let me go.'

'Calm yourself, Mr Simkins. I prefer to find out for myself. Patience, Mr Simkins, patience... Your Miss Hok isn't what she seems. I'm leaving you until she arrives. Relax, Mr Simkins. Don't try anything or you'll join the late Mr Harvey.'

Tim heard the skylight thud shut above him. Cherry would not wait forever for his phone call: she'd be leaving her office at any moment, if she wasn't already on her way.

CHAPTER FOUR

Cherry Hok had tried to control the tension mounting inside her during the afternoon. This was the last day for her yearly annual report: her boss, Cheah Ho Yong, wanted it by tomorrow, and he did not suffer idiots at all. For him, the only animal worse than a human fool was an unpunctual one — and, for the fifth time, she crumpled her final page, 'Recommendations for Improving Narcotics Intelligence', her pet subject. The Investigation Division was barely holding its own, in spite of Mr Yong, its new, ambitious head. This had been a bad year, confirming the suspicion that huge international organizations, political and mercenary, were pouring funds into the lucrative industry of drug trafficking. She glanced at her watch — seven forty-five already, but Timothy had not phoned yet. She was dying to lock up the office and rush down to *Star of Heaven*, but she needed another quarter of an hour to finish her report. She swept back her sleek hair and attacked the difficult page for the last time. The typist would have to make the best of her handwriting.

She sighed with relief: the phone had not rung before she had finished. Cheah Ho Yong would have to like it or leave it — and she flung the rough into the secretary's in-tray. Cherry pushed back her chair, stretched her slim legs as she leaned backwards, and lit a cigarette. Her new boss might be a devil to work for, but he was efficient. Though he and she fought hard over what each believed to be right, Yong had sound ideas. He believed that she was paid to think first and act afterwards, which was why he had moved her out here, to this second-floor office outside the docks. Here she was less tied to the phone, less in the public eye. The drug barons had their spies everywhere, in spite of the thorough screening of all personnel upon which Yong insisted. And Yong and she had unobtrusively begun to infiltrate the ring's underworld: the paying of informers was a dangerous and expensive game, but the swingeing fines and the death penalty for peddling were paying dividends.

Cherry must, now that her marriage to Tim was imminent, tell him frankly of the nature of her work. When their first child came, she would give it all up. For a weak moment she closed her eyes. She loved her quiet Englishman, whose inner strength so few people recognized. Thank the Lord, too, for her father Cornelius, that severe man to whom she was so grateful for her upbringing. She had only to look round at the marriages some of her friends had made to realize how much she owed him, a third-generation Chinese Singaporean man, a Christian of Hakka stock. He had channelled his energy into business, making his fortune during the building of the new Singapore, but he had treated his employees fairly and generously. It was to this quality he owed his success during the dangerous days when the Communists had tried to take over the island.

The Hoks, clever, ambitious and hardworking, had been strict adherents to their Christian faith, and Cherry's father had passed on these virtues to his family; three children had died in infancy, and only Cherry and her brother, Johnny, a pilot on the Harbour Board, had survived. His wife, Leila, had been the rock upon which Cornelius had relied. He had at last consented to Cherry's marriage with Tim, now that he could provide a home in *Star of Heaven.*

Cherry realized she had finished her day. Tim still had not phoned, so she had time to make herself presentable before going down to the sampan. She would lock the cabinets at the same time and be ready for his call.

She applied a touch of lipstick. Her appearance was important in this job. A well turned-out woman was less suspect in the game she was playing, provided she was not too flamboyant. She was almost an 'old' woman at twenty-five, but a satisfactory age: she had negotiated several near-misses in the marriage stakes and she smiled to herself at her memories. Her survival depended on snap judgements and instinctive assessments of people. She would tell Tim tonight of the real work she did — now that they were definitely to share their lives, for he could not be kept on the outside forever.

Cherry locked up. She would leave, even though Tim had not yet rung. She took a final glimpse in the mirror. Yes, she would do: her lime-green skirt fitted well, emphasizing her trim figure. She unbuttoned the top of her shirt, tossed her head and slipped out of the office, locking it behind her.

All the taxis seemed to be booked tonight — one after another they swept past her, back seats occupied. She hated loitering on these pavements, having a sixth sense now of the underworld. Several men strolled past, one of them arrogantly eyeing her from head to toe. He whistled and turned, still watching her. She glanced down, buttoned up her silk blouse — and then she saw an empty cab coasting slowly along the kerbside. She hailed it — a smart job, a white Mercedes. 'The old harbour,' she ordered. 'I'm in a hurry.'

The driver nodded, pushed down his meter. At least it would be a comfortable ride, if expensive. She could not face the bus tonight. She settled back in the upholstery and permitted herself the luxury of allowing her tired brain to wander. The driver was taking the back-street route, probably faster than the throughway, though the worst of the traffic was over by this time. Threading between the rickshaws of Chinatown, they had slowed to a crawl. She lowered the window fully to allow the delicious smells to drift inside.

The aroma of spices, incense and sweat was heavy on the night air. Tourists were already strolling through the teeming streets. Middle-aged Americans in their colourful, baggy clothes mingled with the younger generation, but all shared the same craving — some excitement in their boring lives. The driver was slowly threading behind Sago Street towards Singapore river. Soon it would be impossible to pass, for the street was becoming jammed with tables and dining couples; and later the nightly parade of prostitutes would begin.

Cherry sighed as the taxi drew to a halt in the next traffic jam. This was but the tip of the iceberg in Singapore's vice industry, which thrived in spite of the authorities' efforts. The red lights glowed, the neon signs flickered and flashed, the sex shops and blue films flourished. This was the seamy side with a vengeance, the roots of which her Investigation Division would never unravel or begin to eradicate. Her section, the Narcotics Squad, were realists: it was all they could do to control the worst of the heroin traffic, now that it was flooding through from Southeast Asia after the Vietnam War. Here, in the red-light district, the pushers had it all their own way. She longed to get out of this and find the security of Tim's arms, escape to the other world of wholesome pleasure. Another taxi was hooting aggravatingly behind them and she turned round impatiently.

A kid with a flashing smile had run his bike into the wing of another cab. Through the rear window she watched the angry driver jumping out and shaking his fist at the boy, who was already disappearing into the throng.

Cherry tapped on the driver's partition angrily. 'Can't you take the other way?' she shouted. 'It'd be much quicker.'

He half turned, and she could see the grin beneath his Zapata moustache. 'Okay, missy…' He hauled the Mercedes out of the press and into a side street leading towards the tower blocks bordering the boat quay. Why hadn't the fool taken the other way? She certainly would not tip him — she liked neither his driving nor his manner.

Then suddenly she recalled Tim's remark to her yesterday: she distinctly remembered him saying that he felt he was being held under surveillance … and now she felt the same tingling down her spine. A white Mercedes, he had said; and a man with garish clothes and a Zapata moustache. When she had asked him to elaborate, he had been unable to add anything, except that for the past twenty-four hours he could not shake off the feeling that he was being watched; twice he had seen the white Mercedes, but strongest of all was his sense of being observed and followed wherever he went. The taxi was picking up speed and sweeping down the wide street towards the boat quay and Singapore river.

These years with the narcotics squad had taught Cherry to heed her instincts. When the alarm bells rang, she must act — and swiftly. She leaned forwards and fumbled for her fare as the taxi drew up. She glimpsed the bevy of small craft, then pushed the door handle. As she scrambled out, a bunch of red *canna* lilies was pushed into her face by a toothless old flower-seller. And in that instant, Cherry caught the glance passing between the old woman and the cab driver.

'No, thanks…' Cherry shouted at the flower woman. She walked away swiftly towards the quayside. As she turned, she glimpsed the driver still sitting on his seat. He held a bunch of scarlet *canna* in his hand and was holding it outside the window, moving it from side to side. He stopped when he saw her watching. His face broke into an unpleasant grin.

She was sure now, her senses alert. She hurried along the quayside, away from the sinister taxi-driver. She searched amongst the sampans for *Star of Heaven*, longing for the safety of Tim's calm presence... She could not identify the boat: it was not where she had last seen it ... ah, there it was, sandwiched between the two lighters. Someone was waving from the furthest lighter, but it was not Tim. Strange — and there was no light glowing in the windows as from the other sampans. Then she saw two men, stooped low and scurrying like rats along the side of the craft inboard of *Star of Heaven*.

Her eyes swept along the quayside, across the jumble of bollards and ropes. One of the city police was strolling on his beat around the harbour. Cherry began running towards him. He turned, hearing her footsteps. A look of surprise creased his brown face and when she showed him her identity card, he switched on his walkie-talkie.

'Okay, Miss Hok. I'll collect the next patrol. Then we'll board *Star of Heaven*.' She saw the surprise on his face as he spoke into his mic. She was glad of the touch of his hand on her sleeve while they waited for reinforcements to arrive. She tried to press him towards the gangplanks, but he would not budge.

'We'll wait, if you don't mind, Miss.' His face was serious. 'There's already been one murder here tonight.'

Cherry was used to violence, inured to depravity, but she bit her lip to silence her involuntary cry. She glanced at her watch: it was already a quarter to nine.

CHAPTER FIVE

The deck was deserted when they scrambled aboard *Star of Heaven*. Cherry stood in the corner of the deckhouse, as the largest of the three policemen battered in the doors with his shoulder. She could hear Tim shouting from inside … and surreptitiously she brushed away her tears of relief. Inquisitive neighbours were masking the light from outside, and then she heard the sound of splintering wood. The leader collapsed inwards and the other two policemen followed, pistols in their hands. She scrambled down after them, sick with apprehension.

'Tim … oh, Tim…'

He was crouched in the corner of the saloon. His wrists were bound behind his back, the end of the rope secured firmly to the rail above his head. He stared at her, his eyes wild, as he shouted at the policemen: 'For God's sake, take Miss Hok ashore.' His gaze swung to the half-open lavatory door. 'This is no place for her.' They slashed at his bonds and he was free. He floundered towards her, forcing her backwards towards the smashed doors.

'You're hurting me, Tim.' But Cherry allowed him to push her up the steps, to the night air. Two policemen were crossing the planks and they escorted her gently, compelling her to wait in the police car until Tim had finished in the boat. She felt sick, whether from relief or from the sickly stench in the sampan, she could not be sure. And then Tim was stumbling across the planks, the police close behind. The last of them was carrying a bundle wrapped in a towel. As he climbed carefully ashore, she saw that he was deathly pale.

'The inspector will take you home, Miss Hok,' the sergeant said kindly. 'Mr Simkins is going with you. He'll be making his statement in the morning.'

The lights in the tower blocks were flicking out one by one, by the time Cherry had installed Tim on the cane settee on her balcony. He had remained silent all the way home and it had been difficult to persuade the inspector that he was all right. 'Call us if you need us, Miss Hok,' the policeman had said kindly. 'We'll have a man outside all night.' He had reluctantly driven away. At last, she had Tim to herself.

He downed the neat whisky she held out for him. Cherry watched the pressure evaporating from his taut face, his body slumping on the settee. She knelt beside him, holding his hand. He would talk when he was ready; she remained still, stroking the back of his hand. He was crushing her other fingers and when the pressure eased, she knew that he was asleep. When she saw the purple weals on his wrists, she tiptoed into the bathroom for something to soothe his wounds.

Cherry could watch Tim from here, his shaggy head silhouetted against the indigo of the night. He was shattered by something, yet she did not wish him to talk until he was ready to share the trauma. When eventually he unburdened himself, she would tell him about her job — and probably he would be better able to accept it. She knew now that nothing could separate her from him.

Slipping off her clothes, Cherry snatched the flimsy gown from the hook behind the door and wrapped herself in it. She found the antiseptic, then quietly rejoined Tim on the balcony. She knelt by him and gently bathed his wrists. His eyelids flickered and he watched her steadily, saying nothing, until she had finished.

Cherry did not know how long Tim had talked, lying in the crook of her arm, the softness of his beard against her breast. She let him spill the words, allowed his description of his macabre discovery to spend itself. She barely took in the grisly details, knowing only that he must rid himself of this horror, once and for all time. She stroked his head and when he was silent, she slipped beside him. She joined her lips to his, and as his hands caressed her, waves of pleasure surged through her. She pressed herself to him, feeling for the first time the length of his body on fire against hers. Then, as her hands sought him, she felt him withdraw, suddenly apart. He lay on his back, pressing her head firmly against his chest.

'That's the end of our dream,' he whispered. 'We can't live in *Star of Heaven* now.'

'Of course we must,' Cherry murmured. 'We *must* keep her — she's our home.'

Tim did not reply at once. Then he said, 'Could you live in her? After … *that*?' He had turned, propped on one elbow, so that he could look at her more easily.

Cherry smiled in the darkness, tracing the outline of his lips with her fingertips. 'If we run away,' she said, 'we'll be haunted all our life.'

'Do you mean that?'

'Wherever you live, Tim, I'll be beside you.'

His arm tightened about her. 'D'you understand? I can still see that bloody head…'

For answer Cherry kissed him again, lightly on the cheek. 'Of course I do,' she whispered. 'You'll feel better after we've been to see the boss in the morning. Yong won't let things stand still.'

Tim did not answer. Cherry curled across him and fell instantly asleep.

CHAPTER SIX

The Hoks were seldom all together in the family home outside Port Dickson. Tonight, after Leila's traditional Chinese dinner in honour of the occasion, Cornelius felt a paternal serenity. It was not often he had Johnny and Cherry together, particularly as his son spent most of his time at sea, piloting the stream of shipping through the Straits. Cornelius Hok watched Johnny lighting his cigar, then lit one himself. Cherry's future husband, now sitting in the corner of the verandah with his arm about her, was more subdued than usual. Cornelius was happy about him: he would make his daughter a good husband.

'What exactly did Cheah Ho Yong say, Tim?' Cornelius asked, watching the smoke curling through the meshing around the verandah. Across the dark waters of the Malacca Strait, he regarded the steaming lights of another tanker in ballast passing nor-westwards. The croaking of the tree frogs in the dark garden outside was a friendly accompaniment to the conversation in the candlelight: the flames burnt steadily, without a flicker, in the stillness of the muggy evening.

'Yong was very adamant,' Tim said, looking steadily at his future father-in-law. 'Our experience and Harvey's murder have got to be taken dead seriously. You see … Pop —' Tim smiled shyly — 'I had not realized until yesterday that Cherry was in the Narcotics Division.'

Cornelius watched his beloved daughter taking Tim's hand, as she peered through the cigar smoke at her father. 'I told him last night, Pop,' she said. 'After what happened, he had to know.'

Johnny muttered from the other side of the table, 'You're a close one, Cherry. Damn it, you're marrying the guy.'

Cornelius smiled secretly. He and his wife, Leila, had remained close to each other ever since those early days when he had been sweating it out on the building sites. If it had not been for Leila... He stole a glance from beneath his lids at the woman he had worshipped all his life. They had entered old age together, and a strong bond united them. She was sitting peacefully opposite him, working at her silk embroidery, her silver hair parted down the middle.

'Cherry insists that we keep *Star of Heaven*,' Tim continued, grinning at Cornelius. 'We have paid for her, after all. When we've done her up, we'll soon forget the grisly start. Come down and help us, Johnny.'

Cherry was butting in: 'Yong says he'll move the sampan to Johore for us. He'll have her repainted and given a port of registry. "We won't recognize her," he said.'

'And neither will the secret societies,' Tim added. 'Yong insists that Cherry must lie low for a bit. He's convinced they suspect Harvey split on them, before they butchered him. If they can brazenly do a hatchet job on someone as insignificant as him, Yong wants no risks taken with one of his better agents...' Tim reached for Cherry's other hand. 'And nor do I, Pop.'

Mr Hok met the young man's glance. 'What do you intend to do, you two?' he asked. 'You can't stay in your flat, daughter.'

'We'll take a holiday, Pop. Get right away from the drug scene — disappear from the world for a bit.' She smiled bleakly. 'Difficult, these days, to know where to go, though we've both got our savings.'

'We want to dodge the tourists,' Tim added. 'Cherry wants to show me this part of the world, without becoming involved in the troubles in the north.'

'Ever been to Sumatra?' Johnny interrupted. 'It's a different world. There's a guy running schooner trips to Medan.'

Cornelius felt at peace. Johnny got on well with Tim: as seamen, they had a lot in common. They were swapping telephone numbers and the address of the charter firm.

'How's the work going, Tim?' Cornelius asked. 'Still on that sheep-ship?'

'Slow. We're having trouble installing the fresh water lines. We're having to rip the guts out of her; it would have been quicker to re-build her.'

The old man chuckled. 'You know, I like your topsy-turvy world… Enjoy the paradoxes…'

'What d'you mean?' Johnny asked, sipping his brandy. 'I don't find it amusing. The ships are too bloody big for my job.'

'You shouldn't be a ship's pilot. You should have stayed longer in command.' There was an edge to Cornelius's voice.

'More money in pilotage, Pop. The Straits are hotting up politically.'

Cornelius nodded. He was sickened by the mounting tension in Southeast Asia. 'The ASEAN agreement hasn't solved everything. Lee Kuan Yew was too optimistic.'

'It wasn't his fault,' Johnny said brusquely. 'When it was signed, we were all sincere — Malaysia, Philippines, Singapore, Thailand, Indonesia — we were all for it. We've had enough of being pushed around by the rest of the world.'

'It was the Bali summit that started the trouble,' Cornelius said quietly. 'Checked Japan.'

'Rightly so,' Johnny said. 'I know they've a vital interest in the Straits, but hard luck on them — it's the tankers which destroy our coasts and our fishing.' Johnny was off on his hobby horse again, as he brought Tim up to date. He pushed back his chair and sipped contentedly at his brandy. 'No tanker larger than 280,000 tons can pass through the Straits — and all ships must have a three-and-a-half UKC.'

'What's that?' asked Cherry.

Cornelius was amused by her persistence — or was she just needling her brother?

'Under Keel Clearance,' Johnny said, pursing his lips and glaring at his sister. 'Must have three-and-a-half metres between the hull and the sea bottom, even with squat...'

'Squat?' Cherry insisted. 'What an ugly word...'

'A big ship's stern sits further when she's at speed or even when she alters her speed. God, how ignorant can you be...?'

'Go on,' Cornelius said. 'What else?'

'Deep draught ships, those drawing over fifteen metres, have to use the DWR — Deep Water Route to you, Cherry,' Johnny continued impatiently, 'to avoid trouble in the Buffalo Rock to Batu Berhanti channel. All other ships have to keep out, except in emergencies. The Traffic Separation Schemes apply in the other critical bits — One Fathom Bank, just to the northwest of us here at Port Dickson; the Main Straits and the Phillip channel off Horsburgh lighthouse. Ships mustn't overtake and they're limited to twelve knots.'

A querulous voice spoke from the shadows: 'What do the big ships do, if they can't use the Malacca Strait and the others?'

'That's what Japan are moaning about, Mum. They have to go right round to the Sunda Strait or to Lombok. Sunda is too shallow for the monsters — the ULCCs — so they pass through Lombok and up the Makassar Strait. It's very badly lit and marked.'

'Not so dangerous as the Malacca Strait, Mrs Hok,' Tim said. 'The sand ridges, the deposits brought down by the Sumatran rivers, are the worst hazards. Between here and Pelabuhan Kelang, the Japanese surveyors found transverse sand dunes formed by the currents; some of 'em are fifteen metres high from the seabed.'

'They're always moving, Mum,' Johnny added.

'It must be very dangerous, dear...' The old lady continued with her embroidery.

'Yes, Leila,' Cornelius said. 'It is dangerous. But so are so many things, now that Indonesia's being so difficult. We're acting arrogantly, in my opinion, over our territorial limits.'

'I couldn't agree less,' Johnny said, darting a glance at his father. 'We've got to protect our coasts, even if it means challenging the law of the Freedom of the Seas.'

'Unhappily, our interests clash with those of the Japanese,' Cornelius said. 'Lee Kuan Yew was right about this power in the Pacific, the nation which attacked Pearl Harbor: "This chapter is closed, but not forgotten".'

'That's your generation talking, Pop,' Johnny said. 'We *have* to get on with the Japanese. They don't appreciate having another fifteen thousand miles added to their oil-haul from the Gulf.'

'Puts another thirty percent on transport costs. If Indonesia led the way by closing the Malacca Strait, the Japanese economy would collapse overnight,' Cornelius went on. 'They have to transport all their industry's raw materials.'

'Eighty percent of her oil comes through the Malacca Strait,' said Johnny.

'Oil's *not* her only import, Johnny,' Cherry persisted. 'She must have raw materials for her exports — iron ore from

America, India and Australia; wool from Australia — and fish from all over the world…'

'You sound like a bloody parrot,' Johnny said.

'Shush, John,' his mother said.

Cornelius let them ramble on. He closed his eyes to reflect on these incredible times in which he was ending his life, on the complications posed by the Strait which his drawing-room overlooked…

'Wake up, Pop…'

He heard them chuckling, but he grunted, taking no heed, content with his own thoughts. In the vacuum left by Britain and the other colonial powers, the Southeast Asian nations had begun to flex their own muscles. As a last resort, they could blackmail the superpowers — and Japan — by closing the gateway between the Pacific and Indian Oceans. The Malacca Strait was vital to Russia, to keep open the sea links between her bases in Africa and Vladivostok; and America, too, from her base in Okinawa, needed to watch not only her Pacific neighbours of China, Russia and Japan, but also Africa. Russia, from the Indian Ocean, could, at any moment, cut the oil artery running around the Cape of Good Hope. For the superpowers, the issue was not a matter of life and death, as it was to Japan.

As America withdrew within herself, the vacuum was being filled by Japan — Shanghai was a short distance from Kagoshima. Russia's lifeline to Vladivostok was controlled by Japanese Tsushima in the Straits of Korea, as was La Perouse Strait north of Hokkaido.

Japan's momentum could not be halted; yet she depended entirely upon the timely arrival by sea of her imports — both of raw material and of oil — to maintain her powerful position.

Cornelius shifted his bulk, uneasy with his thoughts: the world certainly had not changed. War was all the youngsters talked about nowadays. And the spectre of a new, militarily powerful Japan was something which he and his generation did not like to contemplate. Japan had ended her American tutelage; she was now treading the tightrope of her destiny. Cornelius sighed.

'What are you groaning about, Pop?'

Cornelius opened his eyes and calmly surveyed his son, imagining him in the near future wearing naval uniform.

'Tim's telling us about his Australian job…' Johnny added. 'His sheep-ship will load at Fremantle.'

'Unfortunate Antipodes…' Cornelius murmured. His cigar had gone out.

The phone started ringing and Cherry jumped up to answer it. When she returned to the verandah, her face was pale.

'You look as if you've seen a ghost,' Johnny said.

'It was Yong,' she said, her voice low. 'My flat's been broken into. They've ransacked the place. I want to go back, Tim.'

Cornelius caught the look which passed between them. 'That's unwise,' he said. 'You'd be better off here.'

Cherry continued staring at Tim. 'Yong agrees with Pop, but he doesn't want me to stay here either. I've got to disappear for a bit.'

'I wish you didn't have this job, Cherry,' Leila murmured. 'Why don't you go up to your uncle's in Kuala Lumpur? You'd be safe there.'

Cherry put her arm round Tim. 'Yong thinks we both ought to disappear for a bit. As Tim's on leave, he's booked a passage for us in one of those holiday schooners to Sumatra. D'you mind, Tim?'

Cornelius saw that her eyes were laughing as she looked down at the man she was to marry.

'How much time have we?' Tim asked. 'I must ring my office.'

'You'll have to be quick,' Cherry said, her face serious again. 'The schooner's sailing at eleven tomorrow, on the morning tide.'

'Where from?'

'Here, at Port Dickson. She's a well-found boat, Yong says, run by a local fisherman. And anyway —'

'And anyway, what?' Johnny snapped. 'You're bloody lucky…'

'I haven't any option,' Cherry said softly. 'If I don't go, Yong won't answer for my safety.'

CHAPTER SEVEN

Jaafar Hamzah revelled in sailing *Bunga Raya* out of Port Dickson harbour. Dodging the sampans and the shipping was exercising his skill to the utmost, as he tacked her across the tideway. His only regret was that he could not give due attention to his passengers, a duty he was forced to leave to the mate, Abdul, whom he had promoted since his father's death. He put the schooner about smartly: he would take her out on a fine reach to the black and white buoy, then harden to the port tack to leave the Bambek Shoal clear to starboard. Abdul could sail her himself to One Fathom Bank, which they should reach just before sunset if *Bunga Raya* continued logging six knots in this perfect breeze. Then he felt the old schooner lifting her skirts as the wind took her into the open sea. For the first time in weeks, he too sensed the surge of freedom. He waved to Abdul, who was talking to the only two passengers they were carrying on *Bunga Raya*'s second 'tourist' trip to Medan.

'She's all yours, Abdul.' He nodded towards the Sumatran coast. 'Watch out for squalls.' The sudden 'Sumatras' were notorious during the southwest monsoon. Jaafar handed over the wheel, checked the set of the sails and wandered from the wheelhouse to the couple seated on the hatch-cover beneath the main boom. The soughing of the wind in the rigging and the hiss under her lee was music to his ears today. He might even make a decent profit with this trip; the holds were packed with Japanese electronics he had picked up at Singapore on his turnround.

'Kind of you to take us at such short notice,' the young woman was saying. She was Chinese but spoke good Malay.

She was smiling. 'My fiancé doesn't speak a word of Malay, I'm afraid; he's English.'

Jaafar shook hands with the red-bearded man. 'I speak English,' Jaafar said, smiling and with hardly a trace of accent. He was lucky with his second batch of passengers: the first trip had been trying, a middle-aged American couple who'd gabbled the whole voyage. He stroked the neat black beard he had grown for his new role, then addressed Miss Hok. 'You've found your cabin? You'll eat with me, I hope?' He chatted with them, putting them in the picture: if the wind held, One Fathom Bank at sunset; Aruah islands, midnight; Sumatra at dawn and an expected time of arrival at 1700 tomorrow evening off Belawan, at the mouth of the Deli river.

'Belawan's on an island, the most important port in Sumatra. Medan, eleven miles upriver, is the fine capital city. It's cool after the mangrove swamps of the coast, but there are some good sandy beaches further down.' Jaafar glanced again at Miss Hok. 'I hope you both enjoy the trip and have a good rest. The weather report is good. I'd be happy for you both to steer the boat if you wish.'

'Thanks.'

The Englishman's face was showing the first sign of emotion. He nodded and grinned and began wandering towards the wheelhouse.

It was a pleasant change for Jaafar Hamzah to share the evening meal with someone other than the crew. As he left the saloon, he was amused by the Englishman, who was hurriedly trying to finish his mango. Simkins rose to follow, taking Miss Hok's hand. 'I'd like to watch you sail her,' he said.

Jaafar entered the wheelhouse and took over from Abdul, as *Bunga Raya* began crossing the separation zones at the entrance to One Fathom Bank.

'I'll get across here quickly,' he told them. 'Too much shipping and too big. They can't get out of our way.'

He ordered the seaman to ease the sheets, and the old schooner was on a broad reach and singing across both lanes. The short twilight had ended when he hardened up for the Aruah islands.

'We'll be sighting Jemur light in an hour or so,' Jaafar told his passengers. 'There'll be a bit of a moon later on.' He watched the steaming lights from the unending stream of ships passing through the narrow channel. He was relieved to have crossed with so little bother: a sailing ship had little chance if she got into trouble. He nodded at the seaman: as the sheets were hardened, *Bunga Raya* leaned again to the wind. 'No need to bother you with the engine tonight. We've a perfect wind.'

The Englishman was pointing to starboard, where a combined white, green and red light was rapidly approaching. A patrol boat, a bow-wave surging at her forefoot, closed from the starboard beam, then sheered off across the starboard quarter.

'She had me worried for a second,' Jaafar grinned at Miss Hok. 'She's one of the United Nations boats that patrol out here now.'

'Who pays for them?' Simkins asked.

'Singapore and Malaysia always used to, but now it's the United Nations. They keep an eye on the shipping to prevent pollution — and they try to catch the pirates.'

'Pirates?' Miss Hok asked. 'Good grief — where do they come from?'

Jaafar nodded towards the west. 'Over there,' he said. 'They attack the sampans and small ships.' He shook his head. 'They're worse than animals, some of them.' In the failing light he drew his forefinger across his throat. He glanced to the rear of the wheelhouse where he kept the old Sten his father had 'won' during the Emergency. 'We've got to protect ourselves now. Things haven't changed much over the years.'

The Englishman picked up the ancient weapon and fondled the shining barrel.

'Careful,' Jaafar said. 'It's loaded.' Simkins carefully replaced the weapon in the corner. 'It's all we've got,' Jaafar continued wearily. 'We don't stand a chance if they catch us by surprise. When they've finished, they vanish into the jungle over there.' He nodded towards the invisible coast of northern Sumatra. 'Piracy's got worse recently. The Indonesian navy looks the other way, with all the trouble between us.' Forgetting his new role, he spat contemptuously through the open window. Then he smoothed his beard then turned to Simkins. 'Like to take the wheel? Steer her as close as you like and we'll be right for the islands.'

Jaafar stayed with his passenger, watching him sail the schooner. The night closed in and it remained very dark until the moon appeared from behind the cloud just before eleven. Jaafar allowed Miss Hok to take her, when Jemur came up, flashing on the port bow. When the islands were clear on the quarter, he would hand her back for the morning watch to Abdul and then Jaafar could get his head down for a few hours. He liked to be up for twilight when it was often foggy. It would probably be dark again, when the moon had set. He wondered when his passengers would turn in: it would be better if they were out of the way when Abdul was on watch.

Jaafar made his way slowly from the wheelhouse. The wind was dying and over to the westward lightning was flickering across the dark horizon. The trip had gone too easily so far and now the night was heavy, brooding, inexplicably menacing. He felt an unease he did not understand, that instinctive warning he had learned to heed, but could never explain. He hesitated, then clambered slowly below.

The patter of feet from the watch-on-deck woke Jaafar at 0340. He lay in his bunk, listening to the foresails being lowered; and then the diesels thumped to life. He dragged himself from his bunk and wearily climbed back to the wheelhouse. Abdul had hauled in the mizzen and mainsheets, and *Bunga Raya* was still making her course. He glanced at the chart, relieved to find that they were still up on their Dead Reckoning. As he moved alongside the mate, he saw the two passengers hovering by the door.

'The engines woke us,' Miss Hok said. 'It's so hot below.'

Jaafar grunted. He did not like the look of the weather ahead — a Sumatra could pounce upon them from the blackness at any moment.

'There's the loom, captain,' Abdul said, pointing fine on the starboard bow. 'Pandang light.'

Instinctively Jaafar timed the flashes — one, every eight seconds. He turned to his passengers. 'That's "The Brothers". Pandang is the northern island. We pass close to the southerly one — Salahnama.'

He crossed to the instrument panel and selected the depth recorder: 44 metres. The schooner must be past the entrance to the Kuala river. He wished he could afford that radar the agent had tried to sell him in Singapore. *Bunga Raya* would soon be approaching the shallows of Jumpul Bank. If visibility did not get any worse, he might pick up the flashing buoy, the black and white conical, off the Asahan estuary. He groped for his binoculars and pushed his way past the Englishman. He propped himself against the doorway and peered through his glasses … nothing, impossible to distinguish even the sea from the horizon.

'How long till twilight, Abdul?'

'Quarter of an hour, captain. Sunrise is 0555.'

Jaafar grunted — five o'clock already. He'd be glad when dawn came. Salahnama was steep-to, protected by a reef with a rock awash half a mile to the southward. He would not see the breaking seas until *Bunga Raya* was on top of the reef, if visibility remained as poor as it was. The moon had vanished, but was that the first sliver of dawn, away on the starboard quarter…? He peered until his eyes ached. A faint lightening was touching the eastern horizon. He stiffened — something else was there, a blur, nothing more… He re-focused the left eye-piece. There *was* something there. Then he saw the phosphorescence of a bow-wave slashing the black water. The boat was darkened, closing fast, and steering straight towards them. Abdul was yelling behind him.

'Captain, port bow…'

Jaafar spun round. Another darkened craft was surging towards them from the misty blur of the landward horizon. As she heeled on her beam ends, turning to port under full rudders, he glimpsed the slim barrel of a gun being trained directly at *Bunga Raya*. Jaafar sounded the alarm hooter, then dashed to the corner of the wheelhouse for his Sten.

CHAPTER EIGHT

Tim hurled Cherry into the far corner and flung himself across her as the first burst swept along the upper deck. He felt the bullets thudding into the wood, heard the windows shattering; he watched the skipper slide, stunned, to the deck, blood pouring from his forehead. As Tim crawled towards the Sten still in Jaafar's hand, he saw Abdul spin the wheel hard over. He then ducked beneath the bulkhead to dive for the gun, which he snatched from Tim. He stood in the doorway, pumping away with the Sten at the gunboat edging up alongside, its aerials still rotating.

Tim heard shouts from forward, then the terrified cries of seamen stumbling along the upper deck. Through the hinge in the doorway, he watched one of them roll to a locker on the port side. The man slammed back the lid and delved inside to extract some old rifles. Several men, doubled beneath the bulwarks, clutched at the rifles as they ran past.

Their attacker, the number '1' painted on her bow, was now so close that the gun-layer could not depress his barrel sufficiently. The captain, wearing a red beret, was leaning across the edge of the open armoured bridge of this sleek craft which bore the unmistakable lines of a warship. He was calmly indicating the targets to his men, when Abdul jumped from his hiding place. He began spraying the bridge, when suddenly his Sten jammed. He hurled down the weapon. He dodged beneath the rail, then began running towards the riflemen now defending themselves from behind the bulwarks.

'Stay where you are,' Tim rapped, forcing Cherry back into the corner. He began crawling towards the Sten which lay on the deck inches outside the open door. There were spare magazines in the rack by the chart table.

The attacking boat was already scraping along the port side, when a jolt thudded his head against the panelling — but now blood-thirsty howls were coming from the starboard side. From where he lay, he glimpsed the crosstrees and bridge of another craft, still rolling from the savage boarding.

Tim stretched out his arms as far as he could, felt the steel between his fingers, then twitched the Sten over the lip of the doorway. Another hail of bullets splattered the woodwork of the wheelhouse. As he rose to one knee, Cherry was crying out hysterically behind him: 'For God's sake, Tim — it's none of our business…'

'They're bloody pirates,' he yelled and he jumped up, shielded by the corner stanchion. He was taking aim with the reloaded Sten on the launch's bridge when he saw Abdul swivel round to starboard to face their new attackers. The old rifle came up to his shoulder, as he aimed at the pirates vaulting across the gunwales. Then Tim glimpsed the captain of the first launch leaning across his bridge. He was taking deliberate aim with his automatic pistol at the back of the mate's skull.

'*Abdul!*' Tim yelled the warning as his own gun began spattering the enemy's bridge. The red beret disappeared. Abdul had fallen to the deck: a stream of blood was running across the planks. The schooner's seamen, seeing their leader struck down, hurled their rifles overboard. Holding their hands above their heads, they cowered behind the bulwarks.

'Get rid of the gun!' Cherry was screaming at him. '*Tim…*'

Tim flung the Sten through the after-port and heard it splash into the sea below the transom. A loudspeaker blared unintelligibly from the first and larger of the two power boats.

Order was being restored on the deck outside, and then there was an unnerving silence. And in that instant, Tim saw that Jaafar was stirring close to his feet. Cherry had slid across the deck and was holding the skipper's head in her lap, when the starboard door burst open. Four thugs burst inside, guns in their hands. They pulled Cherry to her feet, heaved Jaafar upright and, still in silence, dragged them and Tim to the deck outside.

Tim never knew how long the attack lasted — fifteen minutes, perhaps — but twilight was past, and the new sun was warming the deck. Their wrists were bound behind their backs and they were forced against the port bulwarks alongside Jaafar. The crew's survivors, seven of them, were lined up at gunpoint along the bulwarks of the starboard side. It was the silence which Tim found difficult to bear.

Jaafar was whispering from the side of his mouth to Cherry: 'Whatever you do, don't resist. He's the bossman in these parts.'

A tall Indonesian man, tough, lean and smooth-cheeked, was standing before them, his hands behind his back. He swaggered before them, eyeing Cherry. He was wetting his lips with the tip of his tongue when, without warning, he slapped her across the mouth with the back of his hand.

Tim jerked towards him, floundering in his bonds. 'Stop that, you bastard...'

Another blow, this time from the butt end of one of the guards' automatics, and Tim slumped to the deck, his senses reeling. Someone hauled him to his feet. The image of the bully weaved before him.

'And you,' he heard the pirate snarling in perfect English at Jaafar. 'Captain of this schooner?'

Jaafar nodded.

'Where're you bound?'

'Belawan for Medan.'

'What's your cargo?'

'Two passengers…' He inclined his head towards Tim.

'Nothing else?'

'No. Tourist job only. Our fishing grounds are polluted.'

'I don't believe you.' He strutted before his prisoners, the only sound being the idling of the diesels alongside: someone had stopped *Bunga Raya*'s engine.

'You're from Singapore.' He yelled in Indonesian to his men behind him, who loped for'd and began uncovering the hatchway tarpaulin. They smashed the lock, flung back the boards, then vaulted into the darkness of the hold.

Tim heard them talking, and then box after box of electronic gear was heaved up from below. While they were all watching with grim amazement, Tim noticed a twitching in Abdul's fingers. Though mortally wounded, he was inching towards the Sten lying just beyond his grasp…

The pirate chief, one foot upon the coaming, was watching the unloading of the hold. Then he turned to stare contemptuously at Jaafar. He strode towards the skipper. 'I knew you were lying. They call me Tumelaka — ever heard of me?'

Tim saw the gleam in the man's eye. Jaafar remained silent. Before he could answer, things began to move fast.

Abdul lay half upright. A trickle of crimson sloughed at the corner of his mouth and his eyes were crazed in agony. With immense effort he was lifting the gun upwards towards the small of Tumelaka's back, when a guard yelled. Swifter than a cobra's strike, the pirate twisted, falling to one knee, drawing his gun as he dropped. Two shots… Abdul slumped. Tim turned his face away. Cherry was sobbing silently beside him.

His automatic pistol still smoking, Tumelaka, a bizarre figure in his red beret and jungle-green uniform, shouted to a squat, broad-shouldered man standing next to him.

'Execute them.'

The smaller power boat, *Pulau Topang* painted across her stern, cast off to slip slowly astern in the tideway. *Bunga Raya*'s crew were turned about and forced to face outboard, their stomachs cramped over the edge of the gunwale. Starting aft, the hatchet man moved silently behind the first seaman. He pulled out his pistol. Tim could watch no more. He heard Cherry's cry as the first shot rang out. As he looked up, the first victim's feet were being pulled from under him by his executioners. The body toppled into the water, invisible, but Tim heard the splash...

Cherry was crying by his side, but he could do nothing to shield her from the screams, while six more shots followed, one after the other. There was silence, then the laughter of Tumelaka as he spun on his heel towards Jaafar, who was vomiting in the scuppers.

Tumelaka sidled up to Cherry. 'Your name's Hok?'

She nodded, squaring her shoulders.

'You're coming with us.' He nodded again to his sergeant, who padded towards Cherry's diminutive figure. He yanked at her bindings and jerked viciously at the end of the cord. He pushed her aft, towards the plank that had been run out between the two boats. She half-turned, crying out to Tim as she was hauled on board the gunboat — then he could see her no more. The other launch was bumping against the starboard side when Tumelaka faced them again, that evil grin splitting his face. He would be smiling while he slit your throat.

'Listen to me…' He twitched his head towards the gangway. 'Your girlfriend's life is in your hands. You're English, aren't you?'

Tim clenched his teeth and braced himself for the blow, remaining silent. His head swam as a fist smashed into his face. Dimly, he remembered nodding his head.

The voice continued: 'The Red Dragons are holding Miss Hok hostage. You'll be hearing from us.' He barked at one of the guards, then shouted to the captain of the other boat. Tim caught the words 'Raleigh Shoal' and 'Melaka'.

As Jaafar and Tim were bundled across the schooner's deck, Tim glimpsed one of the guards slashing at the lanyards of *Bunga Raya*'s inflatable. Sacks were placed over their heads. They were hauled across to the smaller launch and thrown into the darkness of some compartment below. Someone whipped the sacks from their heads. Tim felt the vibration as the boat's engines increased their revs.

He heard Jaafar calling his name. There was a roaring all about him and then he knew no more.

CHAPTER NINE

Captain Johnny Hok, a middle-aged pilot in the Port of Singapore Authority, had been on the bridge all night on Sunday 14 July. He had been appointed 'additional' to Fast Patrol Boat, *Dag Hammarskjöld*, the second craft of her class in this new Multi-National Malacca Strait Patrol Force. His duties had been precisely defined by the authority: he was to serve in an advisory capacity, an officer 'on loan' to the United Nations Inter-Governmental Maritime Consultative Organization (IMCO).

His job was to assist the commanding officer, Lieutenant-Commander Michael Voon, Royal Malaysian Navy, with the pilotage of his new command in the area, stretching from Horsburgh lighthouse at the eastern end of Singapore Strait to the island of Penang, at the northern extremity of the Malacca Strait: nearly six hundred miles. Hok's appointment was to last a month, when he would resume piloting the stream of shipping through the Singapore and Malacca Straits.

He blinked in the sunlight as he climbed up to *Dag Hammarskjöld*'s bridge. The captain sat in his swivel chair, cool in white shorts and shirt as he puffed at his cheroot. He nodded astern to where the new beacon in the southwest lane of the separation zone, five miles southwest of One Fathom Bank lighthouse, was slipping below the horizon. Voon had passed his opposite number, *Kurt Waldheim*, an identical boat, on opposite course in the channel here during the night. 'I thought I'd make the passage down myself,' Voon said, twitching at his dark glasses. 'Hope you don't mind, Johnny.

You needed a sleep after last night.' He murmured into the helmsman's mic: 'Send up two cups of tea.'

Johnny Hok was enjoying himself, for it was a break to be in a small ship, after the stress of nursing the VLCCs through these restricted waters. *Dag Hammarskjöld* was only 140 feet long, one of Vosper-Thornycroft's boats, but with three Rolls-Royce Proteus gas-turbines, she could knock up forty knots. A sleek job, with fine lines, she was ideal for her role in these waters: her two diesels gave her a comfortable sixteen knots cruising speed, her range being ample for two return trips. The officer of the watch, a lieutenant and Voon's Number One, was steadying for Pyramid shoal when Kelang Radio came through on the loudspeaker:

'*Hammarskjöld, Hammarskjöld — Hammarskjöld.* This is Radio Kelang.'

'I'll take it,' Voon said. 'Come in, Kelang.'

'Good afternoon, Michael: job for you. We've received a telephone message relayed from Singapore. A Caltex ship outward from Dumai has just reported a boat drifting four miles west-south-west of Raleigh shoal. The tanker's laden, so has asked us to investigate. Over…'

'Roger.' Voon nodded at the officer of the watch. 'I should be there in an hour and a half — might just catch twilight. Let me know if anyone gets there first, Bill.'

'Big Head,' Radio Kelang replied. 'Hope our neighbours don't object: you'll be inside their limits.'

'Thanks.' He was chuckling as he glanced at his twin Oerlikons.

'…Out.'

Johnny felt the acceleration as the boat climbed on to her step when the gas turbines came in. The log needle crept up and in seconds she was bouncing along at forty knots. He yelled above the wind: 'Don't depend on the buoy being lit, Michael. Rob Roy Bank was extinguished last week — deliberate interference.'

'Those bloody pirates again,' Voon shouted, nodding towards the westward. 'I reckon their government has plenty of trouble on its hands. Villages in eastern Sumatra have been terrorized for months.'

'Near anarchy,' Johnny shouted. 'No one can control the Red Dragons now — Sumatra's ripe for a takeover.'

'They're worse than animals. They'll do anything to achieve their crazy aims. They thrive on chaos.'

'We've got it here, in the Straits. IMCO's too bloody slow.'

'Indonesia's only paying lip service — even laying her own buoyage system. How *can* the shipmasters cope with the eternal changes and different systems? It's tricky enough for the professional. What about the thousands of sampans? Their skippers can't understand regulations. They've given up.'

The roar of the engines and the wind buffeting the bridge was making conversation impossible.

Voon dipped below the rail. 'It doesn't make things easier — ' he nodded to port as the slab side of a VLCC in ballast, northwest bound, flashed past — 'when none of this stream of shipping belongs to us, to none of the coastal states.'

'Special insurance schemes against oil pollution would help,' Johnny suggested. 'The Oil Giants' Indemnity Fund isn't enough.'

'No one can evaluate the catastrophe of a spill. We've got to cut out the hazard altogether.'

'Impossible — unless we control the Straits like an airport, where compulsion is quite happily accepted.'

'Clear communications are the key to clean water. You know that, Johnny, better than anyone.'

'Sure, Michael, but you need Traffic Control Centres to which shipmasters have to report their positions. We forget what this business is all about…'

Then the naval officer continued thoughtfully: 'Standard procedures worldwide for everyone — that's the only way. Standard communications, a common language, standard emergency procedures, standard targets and even standardized pre-movement intelligence. Route economics, if you like… How often do we give priority to cargoes rather than hulls?'

Johnny had underestimated Voon: this boy had it all.

Voon continued: 'The rules ignore the *raison d'être* for the ship's existence. It's not simple taking a laden VLCC in the dark through an eighty-degree turn round Raffles' light.'

'We'll continue having disasters until we've all got an area mentality. We're just making things impossible for ourselves.'

Voon stood up and pressed the binoculars to his eyes as *Dag Hammarskjöld* swooped across the placid sea. 'Call me in an hour's time,' he shouted to his officer of the watch. 'I'm going below to get on with my report.'

Johnny Hok stayed on the bridge, at this speed happier to be checking the track than killing time below. A sound chap, Voon. Most of the younger shipmasters thought as he did. Johnny idly wondered about the man who was to be his brother-in-law. A reserved bloke, Tim Simkins had spoken little about how to organize things out here — very British, with his parochial view of things. He'd be away soon, on his sheep-ship project.

The sub-lieutenant, who had taken over from Number One, was glued to the radar: 'A small echo off to the southward of Raleigh Shoal, sir.'

'Tell the captain.'

'Aye, aye, sir.'

With Voon back on the bridge, the patrol boat heeled to port as she lined up on the target, now showing seven miles ahead. Minutes later, a tiny speck appeared in the field of Johnny's lenses: 'Right ahead, Michael.'

Johnny was scanning the horizon, searching the low-lying foreshore on the eastern coast of Rupat: there were good beaches between the settlements, where the heat was shimmering above the casuarina trees. He identified the red roof of the large house south of Batu Maung, on the northern side of the Morong channel.

'I'd ease down now, Michael.' Voon was a natural 'coastal forces' man, in spite of his deceptive nonchalance.

Johnny overbalanced as the gas-turbines were cut and the diesels took over. The speck ahead enlarged into the shape of an inflatable. A man was kneeling across the side and waving something.

Dag Hammarskjöld crept slowly up to the rubber boat, the lines snaked across, and then the inflatable was pulled alongside. The survivor, a Malay man by the look of him, had a nasty wound across his forehead and he looked all in. They tried to heave him up, but he refused to move while he pointed to the bottom. Johnny could just make out the body of another man, slumped across the slats. A rope plummeted downwards and the Malay man knotted the bowline around the body. The sailors on deck hove upwards, the Malay man fending off his companion's body until it was level with the gunwale… As the body spiralled in its sling, Johnny glimpsed the mangled face of a European, a cheekbone and the nose smashed in. The face was a mess, the dried blood matting the hair of the bushy, red beard…

Hok felt the kick in his guts; it was Tim Simkins, no possible doubt … but Cherry…? He leaped from the bridge and stumbled down the ladder to the turtle-back of the upper deck.

CHAPTER TEN

During the heat of the summer, Cornelius Hok enjoyed breakfasting early with his wife. At seven, Leila would bring in the batch of newspapers. The routine was always the same: pawpaw with a squeeze of lime juice and a cup of fresh coffee as he cast a cursory eye over the prices on the Singapore stock market. The parrots were screeching in the garden again, but they irritated him little this morning. He and Leila were entering old age together: a serene, agreeable and natural phenomenon. She kissed him and put the newspapers down at his side. He always began with *The Straits Times*. As usual, he counted seven pages from the back…

'Cornelius…'

He looked up.

'Look, dear … the front page.' Her fingers were trembling. She flung *The Times* down on the white cloth before him: *STRAIT PIRACY — PROPERTY MILLIONAIRE'S DAUGHTER HOSTAGE.*

Cornelius sat for a full minute staring at the bold heading. He put his arm about Leila's shoulders, then rose slowly from the table. 'How did they get this information? Why wasn't I called first?' As he walked ponderously towards the telephone, it suddenly began ringing.

'Yes?' He cupped his hand across the mouthpiece and met his wife's eyes. '*Straits Times*,' he murmured. He was at his most formidable when he spoke softly. 'Yes, this is Mr Hok, senior. *You* want to speak to *me*? Look here, young man, if you don't put me straight through to your president within ten seconds, you'll be looking for another job. Get me Arnold Kraal — *at once*, d'ye hear?'

The phone clicked and buzzed, then Arnold's smooth voice was trying to calm him. 'My apologies, old boy, for this appalling mistake. I've sacked the managing editor and was just getting through to you. Desolated to hear about Cherry...'

Hok replied sharply, 'None of your platitudes, Arnold. This is *my* daughter... Where did you get this story? I want every detail. You'd better let me know at once if the kidnappers phone again.'

'Someone phoned through to *The Times* last night, just before we put the paper to bed, and the managing editor passed it. Sounded like a Singaporean. Brazen as hell, demanding half a million dollars. You won't pay, of course, Cornelius?'

The retired property dealer held the phone at arm's length, waiting for the warning signs inside him to subside. He looked at Leila, who was glancing towards the box of pills on the sideboard. 'You haven't a daughter, have you, Arnold?' he asked softly.

'...No. You know Jill and I were not so fortunate...'

Cornelius remained standing, sickened by Arnold's gushing.

'...D'you hear, Cornelius?' The wire was clicking furiously. '...We've been cut off... Operator... Operator...'

Cornelius replaced the phone and took the yellow cachet his wife was holding for him. He gulped the water, swallowed the pill and then the phone was ringing again.

'Yes...?' He was suspicious, ready for the shocks the day was bound to bring. But first he needed a moment of peace, a few minutes in his study for prayers. Leila must be distraught with worry: perhaps she would join him too, after he'd finished with this caller.

'Is that Hok speaking?'

'Yes.'

'Cornelius Hok?' The voice spoke softly, with a distinct, Japanese accent.

'I'm Cornelius Hok... Who's that?'

'We've got your daughter, Hok.' The mysterious voice paused. 'She's safe, providing you do exactly as we tell you.' Cornelius was trying to scribble down the conversation. He needed time, must slow down the talk.

'Who is "we"?' he asked calmly. 'I hold no truck with anonymous threats.'

'Red Dragons.' The voice paused. 'You've got one week to find the ransom. We'll be contacting you in seven days. One week, Hok, no longer, to find the money.'

'How much do you want for my daughter?'

'A million dollars.' The caller laughed shortly. 'She's worth it — what's money, Hok, to a rich man like you?'

Cornelius suppressed his rage. 'It takes time to find that sort of money,' he snapped. 'How can I know you'll return her unharmed?'

'You don't, Hok. We'll give you all the details about where to hand over the ransom next week. Next Tuesday, 23 July. Only a million for Cherry; cheap, isn't she?' The odious voice was chuckling cruelly. 'No trickery from anybody, Hok. Understand?'

'I do.' He hesitated, then asked, 'This isn't a hoax?'

'We're in deadly earnest...'

The phone clicked. Cornelius slowly replaced the instrument. He felt Leila's arm about his shoulders as she led him gently to the verandah.

The head of the Investigation Division, Central Narcotics Bureau, Cheah Ho Yong, had done all he could to prevent the

Hoks from coming into the city to see him. The drive from Port Dickson was too much for them, but the old man had insisted. 'My son's driving me,' he said. 'And I want to see Cherry's fiancé, Mr Simkins.'

Yong had phoned to warn the hospital. Tim Simkins had been cleaned up; miraculously, the damage to his face was superficial, but it was the loss of consciousness that was worrying the doctors. They were going to keep him under observation until they were certain there was no brain damage.

Yong had brought extra chairs into his office. Jaafar Hamzah had a natural dignity as he rose to help the old lady, while Johnny Hok settled his father.

'Mr Hamzah is the captain of the schooner, Mr Hok. They were attacked just here...' He put his finger on the wall chart. 'We've picked up *Bunga Raya*; they're towing her back to Kelang.'

'Is our daughter safe, Mr Hamzah?'

Jaafar did his best, but he could not fool Cornelius Hok. 'When I last saw her, she was all right. But you've heard of Tumelaka, sir? He's always in the news when something particularly odious is going on. He led the attack.'

'What's he like, Mr Hamzah?' The old man was leaning forward in his chair, his head half-turned to hear.

Yong then forgot the morning's work awaiting him. He had never met the terrorist himself, but, whenever the Red Dragons made trouble locally, Tumelaka was behind it, and listening to Jaafar merely confirmed Yong's assessment. Tumelaka was an unstable character, impossible to predict. This latest kidnapping was the worst outrage for some time: human life hung in the balance, in the hands of a fanatic, who was utterly ruthless in pursuit of his aims. It would be difficult to find a more mercurial or dangerous man.

Johnny Hok (Yong had met him twice, once at a pilots' meeting concerning the right of search in the remoter channels; the other, at a staff dinner) laid his hands across his mother's shoulders, while his father concluded his account of the anonymous phone call. Then Yong had to break the painful silence: frankness was the only course with this elderly millionaire.

'If your daughter is not to be harmed, Mr Hok, we must be prepared to bargain and eventually to pay up.' Cornelius's gaze was difficult to meet. Yong lit another cigarette, then haltingly began his assessment of the terrible dilemma confronting them. 'Tumelaka is the most powerful of the terrorist leaders in this part of the world. He and the Red Dragons mean to cause as much havoc as they can, to blackmail society, East and West if need be: in the chaos, they'll grab power... Don't forget, they're run by young, intelligent intellectuals.

'It's no accident that there are millions of young people throughout the world who can't find work — an international disaster, a greater threat to the planet than any military holocaust. That's why Tumelaka and his kind are so dangerous — he crystallizes the dreams of youth who would, if they could, burn all the flags.'

Johnny Hok was impatient, itching to intervene: 'But what do you propose to do? We only want Cherry back — alive and unharmed.'

'We had another message from the kidnapper, direct to police headquarters,' Yong continued patiently. 'Part of their bargain is that we should free our few political prisoners, release those condemned to death at the moment. We've got six peddlers waiting execution, three Red Dragons doing life.'

'More complicated than I realized,' Cornelius said. 'My poor Cherry — and I was once so proud she was working for you, Mr Yong.'

Yong rearranged the trinkets on his desk top. He could not meet the old man's eyes. 'We've a week to find the ransom money, Mr Hok.'

'You can have it tomorrow. No bargaining. Give it to them.'

'Thank you sir...' Jaafar Hamzah had leaned forward, and went on: 'I'm a fisherman, Mr Yong, a humble man from a Malay village. I must tell you that the aims of organizations like the Red Dragons are difficult to resist by people like us: our folk find life very difficult, even when we can fish. When we watch our livelihood being destroyed, we blame the society which seems not to care and is failing us. We see those who govern us getting richer while we get poorer — many can't exist without charity. So when people like the Red Dragons move into our villages, we pay up our "protection" money. Freedom to us is a small price for bread. Liberty is only for the rich...'

The fisherman was speaking without rancour, when suddenly he struck the desk.

'That's how I thought until last Monday, sir. And then I saw the other system at work. I watched them butcher my crew. Quite calmly they did it, just as we gut fish while they're still alive. Last Monday changed everything for me...'

He turned, looking at them in turn, before fixing Yong with his seaman's eyes.

'Take my boat,' he said. 'Sell it. Give the money to Mr Hok towards Miss Hok's ransom. And I've decided while you've all been talking, I'll do everything I can to fight these bastards.' His voice was now unsteady. 'You can use me, Mr Yong, to infiltrate their organization. I look like them. I speak their language. They *must* have a base somewhere in those jungles. We've got to get inside them somehow, if we're to destroy them.'

Yong heard only the whirring of the fan in the ceiling. The old man was the first to speak, as he roughly brushed away the tears from his leathery face.

'We'll make a good team, Mr Hamzah, you and I. We're the same sort.' Then Cornelius turned to Yong. 'Do your thinking, Mr Yong, and we'll co-operate. We've got a week — and someone has to hand the money over when they finally get in touch.'

Yong looked at Hamzah.

'I'll shave off my beard,' the fisherman said. 'I won't be recognized.'

Johnny Hok gave a tense smile as he led his silent mother from the office.

At the door, Jaafar Hamzah turned: 'Please tell Mr Simkins that I'll be up to see him after I've put *Bunga Raya* on the market. He'll help too, Mr Yong.'

The Head of the Investigation Division nodded. He had plans for Mr Simkins, but it was too early yet to reveal them: Cherry Hok's life was hanging in the balance.

The kidnappers contacted Cornelius Hok two days earlier than expected. They caught the old man on the hop, but the message he handed to Yong was succinct and legible: one million dollars and no haggling. The cash was to be handed over by one man only, at an identifiable fisherman's hut on the islet of Pelampong off the northern edge of the Phillip channel — but just inside Indonesian waters.

The time of the handover was fixed for nine, on the night of Tuesday, 23 July. Any signs of an unusual boat approaching the island during the day and the deal was off. The kidnappers would vanish into the jungles as invisibly as they had appeared.

They would return Cherry Hok as soon as the money was in their hands. Yong had arranged for the cash to be handed over in two lots — half a million in the first bundle, the second half as soon as Miss Hok was safe in police hands. The negotiator on the phone had been kept in the dark about this precaution... Yong was certain that, having tasted the fruit, the kidnappers would not be able to resist the whole — and Cherry would be safe.

The problem of Jaafar Hamzah was more tricky. He was calmly determined to get on the inside. He would play it as it came, and he seemed strangely confident he would succeed. He could understand the terrorists.

Yong had decided not to put Tim Simkins in the picture until the last moment — and he would be arriving at any minute for his briefing. This was Tuesday afternoon and in a couple of hours a pilot launch would be setting out for the islet of Pelampong, which lay a mile and a half northwest of Takong lighthouse. Pelampong was of a peculiar reddish hue and was easily approached during the day, there being a landing on the south-eastern extremity of its reef.

The police had suggested encircling the islet in the dark, to capture or to cut off the terrorists after Cherry was safely recovered. The Ministry of Foreign Affairs had vetoed the idea because of the touchiness of the Indonesians regarding their territorial waters. The objective was to save Cherry Hok: but if Hamzah could succeed with his deception, that would be a real bonus. For weeks, Yong had felt uneasy, as if he were tiptoeing on quicksand. So many bits of information were accumulating, none of which meant much on their own: he had seldom felt so restless, and his nerves were tensed to an instinctive receptiveness, an ultra-sensitivity that he knew meant only one thing: his instinct, rarely wrong, was transmitting the warning signals. He sensed some terrible tragedy was at hand. That gutsy Malay fisherman could be the agent by which a trap might be sprung…

A door banged outside and he rose from his desk.

'I didn't think we'd meet again so soon, Mr Simkins.' He indicated the chair while he overtly regarded this man whom he had met last week, after the drug murder in the sampan. Simkins was not so unremarkable as he had first judged. 'You're okay? No fractured skull?'

'Difficult to achieve that,' the Englishman smiled wanly, the corners of his eyes wrinkling. He looked up from the chair across the desk. 'You wanted to see me?'

'Cigarette?'

'D'you mind my pipe?'

'Go ahead.'

Simkins must show a lot more fire in his belly if Yong was to trust him further. Yong could never tell with an Englishman; it was too easy to underestimate them. Simkins was comfortably settled, the plaster across his nose and cheekbone giving him a rakish air as he puffed at his pipe.

'Cornelius Hok is your future father-in-law, isn't he, if all goes well, Mr Simkins? If you don't mind me saying so, he should have bargained with the kidnappers, in my opinion.'

Simkins removed his pipe and stared angrily at Yong. 'If that's what you think, Yong, I'm not interested in your opinion. I thought you had something constructive to suggest for getting Miss Hok back alive. I've got no time to waste with you, as I'm due in Melbourne the day after tomorrow.' He jumped up from his chair and began stomping out of the office.

Yong reached the door. 'Please Tim — if I may use your Christian name — listen to what I've got to say. I have to be certain about you. There's a lot you don't know — and I want you to help us.'

'I'm interested only in getting Cherry back, Mr Yong. We were to marry — can't you understand that?' Resentment was seething beneath the surface. He sat down again, his head jutting forward aggressively. 'If they touch her, harm a hair on her head, I'll spend the rest of my days tracking them down, bringing these bastards to justice. If no one else will, I'll kill them with my own bloody hands — because I'll get 'em, Mr Yong.' And then the spate eased: 'It's Cherry that matters...' He pressed his temples between the palms of his hands.

Yong went to the filing cabinet and took out a bottle of scotch. He poured Tim a glass. 'Here, drink this. It'll do you good.'

He watched the Englishman down the spirit. Simkins looked him in the face, anger gone.

'Okay ... I'm still suffering from these bloody headaches. What are we going to do, eh?'

'You've got to be patient, trust us to do everything we can. Worrying won't help. You've got to keep your job, work normally. That's how you can help.' Yong drew up his chair closer to Simkins. 'I'm certain that all the recent happenings are somehow connected.'

'What d'you mean?'

'The attack on the *Bunga Raya*, Cherry's abduction — yes, and the frightful hatchet job in your sampan — don't they all tie in somehow? I'm certain of it, just as certain that something else is cooking ... and your ship, the *Baitulla*, is involved.'

'*Baitulla*, my old tramp?'

'We've been watching her for weeks, since she began her refit. The owners don't know what's going on.'

'What the hell are you driving at?'

'I've had my boys keeping tabs on her. The hard drug boys have moved in on your ship. We're playing it cool. Millions are involved, if they bring it off. They are using *Baitulla* to carry tons of hard drugs between this part of the world and the Middle East.'

Tim took his pipe from his mouth. 'I've been down to her regularly. They had just finished the fresh water lines and the sheep pens, before I took the schooner trip.'

'They've been clever, infiltrating the fitters and welders, paying big money. Rows of watertight lockers have been fitted below the strainers — deep down in the bilges. The sheep muck will cover the lot and no one will relish looking there. There's enough stowage in the lockers for half a ton of drugs: but they're not loaded at the moment — that's where you come in, Tim.'

'Me?' Simkins sat up. 'I hope to be doing one trip only. I'm appointed as her chief officer, until her permanent mate is well enough to join us. He's in hospital in the UK with jaundice — for a couple of months, they think. But what do you want me to do, Cheah?'

'To know nothing, but to keep a close watch on things. I must know where the drugs are loaded, how they enter the ship. It's a gamble, but if we can grab the stuff and the middlemen, we could snatch the ring and catch the big boys.'

'How does this help us get Cherry back?'

But even now Yong could not risk compromising Jaafar Hamzah — and the Malay man had not succeeded yet. 'The profits go directly to the Red Dragons. They may even be the organizers. If we hauled in some of their top men, we'd be in a strong position to trade her for some of them…'

Tim Simkins' face had set in hard lines. He got up and held out his hand. 'Okay, Cheah.' He began easing towards the door. 'How do I communicate with you if I discover anything?'

'Don't: too dangerous and too long. Ring my office if you can; otherwise, telex.'

'I'm flying tomorrow. And Cherry?'

'You'll hear from me at once. An innocuous message from your yard here, addressed to Mr Simkins. A positive statement will mean she's safe.'

'And a negative…?'

Cheah clasped Tim's hand. 'We shan't know for another day or so, Tim. I'll ring Fremantle at once.'

He accompanied the Englishman to the doorway of the block. He watched him until he was lost in the crowd pouring through the gate for the afternoon shift.

CHAPTER ELEVEN

'Stand by, Mr Hamzah.'

The police inspector shook Jaafar's hand, then led him aft, towards the davits of the rubber inflatable. Five minutes earlier, the launch, one of the improved P6s, had reduced speed as it neared the dark smudges of the Takong islets. The skipper rounded up to place the Raffles light dead astern. The night was glassy calm and the only sound was the hiss along the waterline.

The launch was still in the obscured sector of the Takong group's flashing light. In a few seconds, she would be crossing into the white sector, when the gleam of the light's beam would make the islet of Pelampong even more difficult to see. Jaafar felt the power coming off the engines and then the boat was losing way, rolling gently to the wash from the VLCC which was passing to the north of them; she was less than a mile and a half distant, her port light fading and her stern light coming up.

'See the islet, Mr Hamzah?'

'Directly ahead, five hundred metres off.' The low-lying lump of rock, a few trees perched sparsely upon it, was illuminated every ten seconds by Takong's white beam. The pale circlet of surf curled lazily upon the reef stretching to the westward.

'Got everything: red torch, mini-flares — and an extra lifejacket for Miss Hok?' the inspector asked. 'The two money sacks are in the dinghy, both buoyed with twenty fathoms of line. Constable George will look after you, Mr Hamzah — he's one of our best marksmen and a trained diver.'

Jaafar climbed into the rubber dinghy. The dark figures above him were silhouetted against the glow from the flickering buoys and the lighthouses.

'I'm ready,' he murmured to George. He heard the painter plop across the rounded bow, then felt the dinghy ease forwards towards the surf which seemed much closer — he could hear, above the coughing of the outboard, the waves breaking against the rocks. George approached close, then turned to port, keeping parallel with the reef until the gap in the white ribbon showed. He throttled back, nodded to Jaafar.

Jaafar moved his weight forward, stretched wide his arms across the gunwales. Though his heart was pumping hard, he felt calm now — he had said his goodbyes at home and was at peace with himself... Khadija was a fine wife and had tried to understand.

'Jump, Hamzah.'

The rubber boat was scraping against the concrete slab which fishermen must have laid for their solitary landing place. He slithered over the side and splashed through the warm water as the dinghy went astern to wait twenty metres offshore. He raised his hand and then strode towards the trees.

Jaafar did not hear the surf breaking behind him, nor the beat from the tankers' engines as they passed slowly up the Phillip channel, less than two miles to the southeast. He was keyed to his highest pitch, his eyes probing as the lighthouse beam flooded the islet, bright where the light caressed the flat surfaces, very dark in the shadows. Nothing moved. He walked steadily towards where the huts should be: they had been described in detail over the phone to Cornelius Hok. The furthest of the five huts, they said, on the northwest tip of the islet which was only 150 metres long... He could hear only the soft padding of his own footsteps across the soft soil — that, and his heart beating.

Jaafar sensed the invisible eyes watching him, waited for the flash of a gun, the thud of a bullet in his back … and then he saw the four inflatables lying across the tidal stream, dipping in the swell to the westward, the outline of a man in each. A row of huts detached itself from between the trees — there were five and the furthest were separated from the others. He walked slowly towards them.

All was still while Jaafar passed the first hut, an affair of bamboo and banana leaves. The open doorway was a black rectangle … and then he saw a shadow gliding between the huts. His grip tightened on the sack lashed to his wrist. He slipped the knife from his sleeve, felt the hasp in his palm. He walked slowly onwards, past the third, then the fourth hut. He halted, within a metre of the last one.

'Miss Hok…' Jaafar called softly. He listened. No movement, silence — save for the whisper of the waves washing across the reef. The men in the boats were watching him; but he could not see the ghosts behind the trees. The beam from the lighthouse flared intermittently, throwing up grotesque shadows around him, shadows that danced like puppets. He spun round, sensing the hidden watchers. From both sides of the hut, three black shapes detached themselves, pistols aimed directly at his guts. He stopped rigid, even as he felt the snout of a gun in his back. He flexed his muscles, waiting for them to grab the sack.

'Who are you?' the man behind asked sharply. 'You're Malay?' He spoke with an Indonesian accent Jaafar could not identify — nor could he recognize the hoarse, arrogant voice. None of those gunmen, masked below the eyes, was tall enough to be Tumelaka. He felt as if his arm was being pulled from its socket, as the man behind him jerked fiercely at the sack.

'I didn't want this job,' Jaafar shouted angrily. 'I'm only the go-between.' He jerked his arm free. 'Show me Miss Hok first.'

One of the terrorists muttered something behind his mask, and a figure stumbled out of the detached hut; even in this feeble light he recognized Miss Hok, his recent passenger in *Bunga Raya*. She looked much slighter and more bedraggled. Her hands were bound behind her, attached to a length of rope which one of her captors was holding. She was mouthing incoherently and her eyes were wild. 'Take me away. Oh, take me away,' she sobbed quietly, her eyes sweeping over him. If she had recognized him, she had given nothing away — shaving off his beard shocked even his wife. Miss Hok stood swaying in front of him, held firmly by the rope.

'Hand over the money,' the harsh voice behind him snapped.

'When Miss Hok's in the boat.'

'We don't move until we have the money.'

Jaafar knew that this was the moment of crisis. He unsnapped the fastening at his wrist, then tossed the sack to the ground.

'How much there?' the leader growled behind his back.

'Count it. Five thousand hundred-dollar notes.' Jaafar held his breath. The gun barrel in the small of his back poked viciously.

'That's only half... Where's the rest?'

'In the dinghy. You'll get it when Miss Hok's on board. Give me her rope.'

The man behind him hesitated. Then he shouted, and the rope was flung across. Jaafar caught it, waited for the grovelling men on the ground to finish their count.

'Five thousand total,' one man grunted. 'Half a million dollars.'

They were muttering amongst themselves, then their leader spoke sharply behind him: 'Try anything and we'll kill you both.'

'That's why they sent me. I'm expendable,' Jaafar blurted out. 'I'm out of Changi jail for this job. Give me Miss Hok and let's get this over with.'

'Get going...' The gun prodded hard as the rope was shoved into his hand. Jaafar shortened the wire-stranded cord which was cutting into the sobbing woman's wrists. 'Keep close to my side,' he told her. And as he moved forward, he half-turned, and shouted at his guards: 'If you touch Miss Hok again, the launch will open fire on the lot of you. They won't bother about me.' He laughed bitterly.

'We shan't worry about either of you once we've checked the second half,' the leader said. 'You'd better be right...' The clearing by the landing place was opening before them. 'Go on ahead — *now!*'

Jaafar held the rope tightly. 'Walk ahead of me, Miss Hok, then get into the dinghy.' The rubber boat was edging towards the concrete hard and he heard the outboard chuffing as George brought her in. Against the loom of the lighthouse beam, the dark silhouette of the police launch was visible, its bow and Oerlikon guns pointing directly at the hard. 'Into the boat,' Jaafar told her softly.

Miss Hok began splashing through the water. As he gave her slack, the rope was wrenched from Jaafar's hand.

'Not so fast,' the thickset terrorist hissed. 'Not till we've counted the money.' The thug shoved Jaafar forwards. 'Get the cash.' He was jumpy, now under the glare from the lighthouse, and exposed to the police launch. Jaafar suddenly felt confident — Miss Hok was almost safe, where she sat trembling on the edge of the dinghy.

'Here you are, Jaafar…' George's voice, calm and matter-of-fact, snapped the Malayan fisherman back to reality — but one slip and anything could happen. His nerves were raw and he wanted to yell his lungs out, to release the unbearable tension… He sloshed back to the beach. He tossed the sack at the anonymous thug's feet. Someone grabbed him, held him while they emptied the dollar bills on to the dank soil. He would never forget the grotesque scene: ten men, each counting the bundles of 100-dollar notes, scrabbling on the ground and muttering between themselves. As each man finished, he reported his total.

But the ninth man was shouting: 'Ninety-eight only,' he said. 'Ninety-eight…'

'Count again,' the boss growled. 'Hurry — let Salim count.'

The favoured guard grabbed the deficient bundle and began counting aloud. An excited argument was developing, while all eyes watched the vital count … and Jaafar surreptitiously glanced toward the dinghy, riding gently in the swell. George, apparently absorbed by the final count, had slipped beside Miss Hok. His head jerked upwards from time to time, watching the weaving gun barrels — but then Jaafar saw his other hand. It was masked by Miss Hok's body, but Jaafar caught the glint of a steel blade at the prisoner's rope, slicing, sawing, backwards, forwards, backwards, forwards… *For Allah's sake, it's wire-stranded — you'll never get through it*, thought Jaafar. *They're a trigger-happy bunch, George — and we're so nearly there…*

'Seventy-one, seventy-two…'

The man they called Salim was bent low, his companions crouched round him. The leader was watching, his head weaving from side to side, his pistol finger crooked around the trigger... Then suddenly there was a commotion in the rubber boat. George had overbalanced, falling forwards... In trying to save himself, his knife blade was visible — and then they spotted the rope, half chopped through, the splayed wires glinting in the weird light.

The boss-guard, already twitchy, leaped backward, tugging at the rope. Miss Hok jerked, shrieked, then tumbled backwards into the water. Floundering to her feet, they hauled her across the concrete. A nervous guard began pumping bullets into the defenceless George, who slumped backwards across the outboard's tiller. Another man splashed through the water and ripped the inflatable along the waterline. Jaafar yelled at them: 'Run, for God's sake! The launch'll open up.'

He remembered little of the next few minutes — only that Miss Hok was being slung between two men and that he was stumbling after them, being jabbed in the back by hard steel. Bullets began whipping through the trees, dirt flying in their faces... He flopped into one of the waiting boats, heard the engines roar as the small flotilla threshed across the edge of the reef. He saw the frenzied figure of Miss Hok, her legs kicking over the gunwale of the boat ahead ... and then they were across the sharp coral and bouncing through the eerie glow of the red sector; hurtling past the surf of Takong Besar island, then Little Takong with its lighthouse towering above them ... out into the Phillip channel, cutting across the snout of a VLCC in ballast, shaving the gleaming sides of a black conical buoy with its regular three flashes...

Someone was astride him, sitting on his chest, and Jaafar could not breathe while the inflatable bounced across the sea, pounding the air from his lungs. Then they were in darkness, but soon the loom of land was coming up on either bow. The police launch had vanished. In their exultation, the boat's crew were yelling their heads off in derision, while they wildly fired their automatics skywards.

Jaafar struggled free from the man on top of him. The wind slapped him in the face as the boat careered, last in the weaving line, up the channel between two low-lying shores. Groups of huts on an island whipped past them, so they must be somewhere between the islands of Bulan and Kapalajernih, where he and his father had sometimes fished.

Jaafar was in the hands of a bunch of madmen and disappearing into mysterious country where the force of law had scarcely reached the interior. Miss Hok was still alive, but he had little hope now for himself, once his captors' euphoria had worn off. Miss Hok was still of immense value to them, for although they had already got the cash they could still try to extract more ransom money. He had only one chance — and he shouted at the top of his voice as he saw the luminous sheen of an underwater rock ahead. The coxswain put his helm hard-over, the boat sheered violently, then tore on blindly, up the channel and into the night.

CHAPTER TWELVE

The dry heat of Perth was a relief after the humidity of Singapore, but Tim could not reach Fremantle quickly enough. The flight had been uneventful, but *Baitulla* had reached the port of Fremantle only two days before his arrival. He was glad to see her ugly shape, lying on the sheep-loading jetty, close to the rail sheds where the 'rakes', as the sheep trains were called, would be arriving in six days' time, crammed with 25,000 sheep from the sheep stations. This grubby old tub, transformed from its original freighter role, was real, something he could understand amidst the nightmare of the past ten days — and there must be news from Yong awaiting him…

Tim paid the taxi-driver and staggered with his bags to the gangway, where he paused for a moment to regard his temporary home for the next few weeks. She had been freshly painted in her new colours, but the rust marks were already showing through the grey. The letters of her new owners were painted in bright orange along her sides, AST, a recently constituted company calling itself Arabian Sea Traders which had entered the rapidly expanding and lucrative business of shipping live sheep to Saudi Arabia.

Baitulla had put in for a day at Surabaya to bunker with cut price fuel and to take on stores. She passed through the Lombok Strait, then caught the dusting on her passage down to Fremantle. Gazing up at the old ship on which he had taken so much trouble in Singapore, he was thankful now that her mate had gone sick: this job was a diversion that would tax Tim to the limit while the agony of Cherry's abduction was being played out, a drama in which he would have gone crazy as a helpless onlooker … and Yong had given him a vital task to perform. He picked up his bags and struggled up the gangway.

A harassed, capless officer was approaching down the deck, a sheaf of papers in his hand. He smiled, introduced himself as the second mate, then helped Tim down to the chief officer's cabin. 'I'm Stefan Daniolos. There's a telex on your desk, sir. I'll take you to the captain when you're ready.'

'Give me a few minutes.'

Tim dropped his bags and drew the curtain across his cabin door. He tore open the envelope lying on the desk: *From Mr Yong, PSA, to Mr T. Simkins, SS* Baitulla, he read. *Reference recent enquiries, regret negative, repeat negative results. Efforts are continuing and it is hoped objective will be achieved successfully. Contact PSA earliest. Signed: Yong.*

Tim subsided into the chair. He needed time to collect his thoughts: he would shift into uniform and report to the master, then go ashore to find the nearest phone.

Timothy Simkins paused outside the door to the Master's State Room, on which a card was fixed: *Captain Klaus Rittel.* He knocked, and hearing no reply, he opened the door. Gazing through a scuttle was the large figure of the master, in white tropical rig of a short-sleeved shirt with epaulettes, and baggy shorts. He was bare-legged and was wearing sandals. When he turned, Tim sensed that he had seen that heavy face before. The master, his eyes bleary with weariness, was regarding him with faint amusement.

'Soapy Simkins,' he said, unsmiling. 'Why does it have to be you?'

Tim suddenly recognized him but said nothing. He stared at Rittel until the bully of their boyhood was forced to avert his eyes. 'Why have you changed your name?' Tim asked. 'Wasn't Hosea good enough? We'd heard you'd gone to the States.'

Rittel turned angrily. 'My father's decision. I got my ticket there. I've been working out here ever since.' He advanced towards his temporary mate. 'I know this part of the world, Soapy. Just do your job, that's all. I'll remind you I'm the master and my word goes.' He nodded towards the fo'c'sle. 'In five days' time, twenty-five thousand sheep will be spilling from the rakes. Your job's to load and look after them. Mine's to get the ship to Beirut.'

Tim was seething, but he had nothing to lose. 'The less we see of each other the better,' he said. 'I don't suppose you've changed much, sir. You may be three years my senior, but you can't make my life a misery here, as you did in nautical school.' He looked him straight in the eye. 'I'll run your ship for you until my relief gets out here.' He turned, slammed the door behind him, and hurried to the upper deck for air. His head was swimming from suppressed rage and the headache was throbbing again in his temples. He walked slowly aft to the poop deck, where the second mate and several of the mixed Malay and Arab crew were chatting to a grey-haired, swarthy Arab man.

'The bos'n,' Daniolos introduced, 'Ghazzan Massan. Our new chief officer, Ghazzan…' The bos'n touched his forehead.

'Only for this trip,' Tim said, watching the reaction of Ghazzan. 'I'm only with you until your permanent mate joins us. Can you take me round the ship, bos'n? I helped fit her out in Singapore. I'd like to see what you've done to be ready for Tuesday.'

'Right, Mister Mate, sir. Captain told me you were coming. We'll start for'd on this deck, then work down to the pens and bilges.'

'Give me an hour, Ghazzan,' Tim said. 'I've got to go ashore first.'

The art of telephoning, Tim had discovered during his wanderings, was always quickest from a modern hotel. And as he waited impatiently in the plush lounge for a line to Singapore, his mind whirled around the day's developments. He idly watched the assortment of passing travellers criss-crossing the reception hall, each intent on his own affairs — the more affluent they appeared, the more worried they looked.

The sheep-ship job was tough enough to take his mind off his anxiety about Cherry, but to be afflicted with Rittel as master of *Baitulla* was a cruel twist. Serge Hosea, bully of the James Cook Nautical School, had always been jealous of the younger Simkins, since the first moment they shared the same maths set. Hosea was not a brainy kid, and resented Simkins' success; he was a slight, shy boy in those days, detesting games and the physical training meted out to the aspiring mariners. Until Hosea's departure from the school, life for Simkins had been miserable...

'Your call to Singapore, sir.'

Yong was on the line. 'I'll make it short,' he said. 'This isn't a closed line...' and Tim had to fill in the gaps as Yong described the abortive ransom attempt. 'We've had contact with the opposition,' Yong continued. 'They're demanding more money.'

'Is she...' Tim said softly, 'is she still alive?'

There was a pause, then Yong said, 'All right ... yes, she's okay. I heard her on the phone, that's how I know. I asked about the fisherman. She had seen him once — nothing more. They're trying to blame the failure on us. They hold all the cards at the moment.' Then he changed the subject. 'Keep in touch… Yes, I'll let you know at once. Do the same for me.' The line clicked — that was it — and Tim walked back to the ship for his first meeting with Ghazzan.

The weekend in Australia was somewhat different from those in the dockyard of Singapore, for in spite of the attractions of double-time and other benefits, it was sacrosanct. The quay was deserted and *Baitulla*'s officers, including the master, had gone ashore. Ghazzan had promised the boys a run, and though they wouldn't be drinking, they'd be finding other pleasures.

The gangway quartermaster was snoozing in the shade thrown by the overhang of the boat deck. Tim walked quietly across to the other side.

The darkness on the main sheep-deck, even with the police lighting, was a contrast to the glare of daylight on deck. Tim walked past the pens, taking the route that the sheep would follow in a few days' time. Sections A to D had been finished, but the fitters were still finishing off the pump strainers and the last of the pens in E and F. He walked aft, along the gangway wide enough for a single sheep, to the large open space of D section, and switched on the fluorescent lighting.

They had done as he'd asked, welding the new pen catches on to the outside of the enclosures. The pens looked fine, the decks clean and fresh, the drains uncluttered where they led to the strainers feeding the pump suctions. Tim walked aft, to the farthest corner on the starboard side. He lifted the plate above the pump suction to the main sheep drain. Clean as a whistle. The fitters had finished there, but one of the deck plates had not been replaced properly. He lifted it upright and peered beneath it.

At first he could see nothing in the gloom. He shone his torch into the bilges; the smell of the red oxide was strong and it could not have been long since this had been painted before shutting down the plates. His adrenalin began coursing as his torch picked out another shape, something alien to the bilge round. He counted six zinc-plated lockers in a row, each rectangular and about eight metres long. Each had a hinged front and was padlocked — and there was the same arrangement on the other side: clever, just above the bilge water, even during a list, yet below the decks of the pens which would soon be a mass of matted filth. Tim stepped back and replaced the deck plate, leaving it exactly as he had found it. He resumed his tour of the sheep-deck, saw that they might be ready for Thursday, then returned to his cabin. He needed privacy to think.

When he had closed the door behind him, he felt a strange unease. This trip would be no picnic. In addition to getting the sheep safely to Beirut, he had one priority only if he was to help Cherry: he must keep his eyes skinned. Who was in this dangerous racket? And if he could find out, and get back to Singapore alive, he'd have to watch his step…

It was late the next day, Monday, 29 July, when Tim first heard the sound — and it would remain with him for years after he had left the ship. The eternal bleating of sheep, the baaing that would drive the crew demented. The first of the sheep wagons had clanked to a stop in the unloading bays.

Tuesday was hot and sticky, even at dawn. Tim had finally turned out, unable to sleep, to savour the cool morning air before the smell of sheep became a part of life. He paced the poop deck, while waiting for the Australian officials.

The oil riches of the Arab nations had produced one curious spin-off — this trade in live sheep, a bonus for a shipping company such as his own. With commendable speed, *Baitulla* had been converted from general cargo and sold as a sheep-ship to Arabian Sea Traders, who were to pay London Shipping for managing and manning AST's sheep-runners. In the newly rich Muslim countries, the demand for live sheep had already exceeded supply.

Until recently, mutton and lamb destined for the Arabian Peninsula had been killed in Australia and New Zealand by certified slaughterers, gentlemen of the Muslim faith. The Muslim religion required that a prayer to Allah must be invoked while killing an animal for meat. Each mutton and lamb carcase had to be certified as complying with this requirement, before being loaded in refrigerated ships for the Arabian Peninsula. If the live animal could be slaughtered in the Arabian Peninsula, not only would the meat be of better quality, but there would be no risk of the religious ritual being ignored. The sheep trade might seem callous, but now that the Arab nations could afford the luxury, it was becoming a money-spinner for the Australian sheep farmers.

At last, Tim could see movement down on the quay. At 0743, the first sheep emerged from the rakes, the first of 25,000 wethers controlled and checked by government inspectors.

The ship's officers had taken up their positions; the shepherds waited on the open decks. Then the rail car spilled the first of its sheep, herded by the snapping, barking dogs. The handlers were yanking out the first protesting animal, shoving it onto the ramp which led down into the ship's hold. Like a string of beads, the bleating, confused animals followed, at five hundred an hour, all day long. By the end of the morning, the heat of the sheep in their pens below had pushed up the temperature. The ventilation fans roared, but the stench of stale ammonia began to infiltrate everywhere, to saturate the atmosphere, until, finally, they all became inured to the stink.

By the end of the second day, all on board suspected that sheep were the dimmest, most obstinate, feeblest animals God had created. By Wednesday, the suspicion was confirmed. Hour after hour, the sheep plodded up the ramps, bunched at the corners, panicked in the narrowest bottle-necks. Pulled and goaded, the pens gradually filled up.

On Wednesday afternoon, Tim saw one of the Sudanese stock-men hauling a dead sheep along the deck. Before Tim could stop him, he had opened the off-side shell door and calmly pushed the body over the side. Within minutes, an inspector from the Health and Quarantine Department had stormed on board. He summoned more of his team and threatened to quarantine and stop the ship.

It took all Tim's persuasion to alter their decision. A tug was summoned to recover the bloated corpse floating in the harbour. It was towed alongside, a rope was passed round it and the dripping, soggy sheep was hauled up to the rail. As it was manhandled over the side, the body was squeezed against the rail. The handlers fell back from the disgusting stench as they plopped the corpse into the scuppers. It did not take long for everyone to realize that under tropical conditions, the stench of a decomposing sheep was overpowering if it was not dumped within hours of death.

The ship was working in two watches, day and night, but the rake of rail cars seemed endless. And the more tired the men became, the more stupidly the sheep behaved. Unless kept continually on the move, they would bunch and fight to turn back, forming solid wedges. And the more the exhausted men tried to move them, the tighter the sheep would pack into one another.

But by Thursday evening, on the first of August, the last three rail cars hove in sight and the ship's warps were singled-up. Tim climbed wearily to the master's cabin.

'Ready for sea, sir.'

Rittel glanced at his watch and reached for his cap. Without a word, he walked past his chief officer and clambered up to the bridge.

CHAPTER THIRTEEN

The ship and her crew quickly settled down, thankful to be at sea at last. Watering and feeding the sheep filled working hours, but every day the pens had to be checked for dying and dead sheep.

Making seventeen knots, *Baitulla* reached the tropics on Sunday, 4 August — and with the heat accumulating from the sheep's woolly bodies in the decks below, in spite of the ventilation fans roaring at maximum revs, the animals began expiring at an alarming rate — up to thirty-eight a day. As many sheep as possible were moved up and barricaded on the upper deck in the air. The three evaporators were designed to provide forty-five tons of water each per day, but they were falling short of their designed production.

On 9 August, eight days out, fifty dead sheep were dumped over the side, their bodies floating astern like a string of bloated balloons. Then the chief announced that the forward empty fresh water tanks were not accepting water from the distillers; and that his overworked engine-room staff could not remedy the fault.

Sheep were dying hourly, so a fire hose was rigged from the boiler feed connection along the deck and into the sounding pipes of the sheep tanks. But the price of maintaining an adequate supply of water was high: the humans had to forgo the luxury of washing.

Then the pumps refused to suck the urine and liquid excreta from the sumps — and this was when Tim discovered an unexpected ally in Ghazzan, the bos'n.

'The strainer plates are choked in the pens, sir,' he reported. 'Before I could stop them, the stockmen lifted the lids of the pump chambers and got rid of the shit by heaving it down into the bilges. The pump has run dry and cut out. The spilt drinking water in D hold is slopping about, because it can't drain away. The sheep are up to their knees in it.'

'We'll have to clear D and shift the animals on deck,' Tim said, 'or the humidity will kill the lot.'

Ghazzan nodded, sucking his teeth. 'We'll have to be quick about it, sir: fifty-five today.'

'Okay. Call out everyone. I'll tell the officers.'

'You can leave the clearing out of the bilges to me, sir.' As he turned to leave, Ghazzan added, 'The lads have had a bellyful of this, sir.' He was still mumbling to himself as he disappeared down the passage. A recent rain squall cooled down the scorching deck. It did the hands good to watch the sheep, sniffing the breeze and enjoying the dampened wood… Then the wind backed. With no relative wind, even on deck the sheep began to suffer, so Ghazzan rigged awnings for them, using old draw sheets and tarpaulins.

The sheep then chewed the frapping lines until he moved the ropes above their heads. The stern light then refused to work: the chief's language at supper was worse than usual — some monster had nibbled through the light's electric cable, shorting the circuit. To complete Ghazzan's day, the wind veered back to its original quarter, so his awnings had to be furled. When tempers had reached breaking point, 'Sparks' handed a message to the master. *Baitulla* was to alter course for the Persian Gulf: the fighting in Beirut had broken out again.

On Friday, 9 August, they sighted Gan, the one-time RAF staging post at the southern tip of the Maldives, on Addu Atoll. Spirits rose, for the chief discovered non-return valves in the duct keel, valves which had been there since the ship was built — and so the supply of fresh water to the sheep tanks was resolved; and then the miracle was discovered in E Lower Tween Deck. Ghazzan emerged, a wide grin on his face, with a new-born lamb in his arms. Even Rittel was affected, declaring it should be the ship's pet. The sailors built a shelter on the poop deck for the mother and its lamb. From then onwards, some soft-hearted sailor was always hovering by the feeding trough to administer to the pair.

Tim was on the bridge when further orders came in: *Baitulla* was to proceed to Beirut, after all. His heart sank — another four days to Suez — and just when the Persian Gulf was coming up from below the horizon. The daily death rate was now in the fifties, and any further delay would be tragic.

The captain grunted as he passed the signal to his mate. 'At least we shall see signs of civilization again,' he said. 'We'll be entering the shipping lanes tomorrow.' He was lounging back in his chair, cooling himself with an ancient moon-shaped Shanghai fan. His shirt was pulled open and amongst the black fuzz, Tim noticed a key hanging from the silver chain about his neck. Rittel was looking up at him antagonistically. 'How many dead today, Mr Simkins?'

'Fifty-four, sir. But the smell's getting worse. The bos'n reckons we've over three hundred tons of manure to shift.'

Rittel remained silent, staring across the smooth sea to the horizon. Tim wondered what the death rate would have been if they had encountered bad weather.

At last, the red mountains of the Arabian Peninsula slid past them to the northward, and *Baitulla* anchored in Suez Bay. The cessation of the old ship's vibration and the sudden peace was a boon for jagged nerves. Then a further signal was received: the ship was to remain at anchor in Suez Bay and await orders

— once again, the ripples of the Beirut tragedy went spreading wide.

The chief entered Tim's cabin and slumped in his overalls onto the bunk. 'We'll *have* to weigh anchor this evening, Tim. We've only just enough water for the sheep tanks,' he said. 'We'll have to get underway to run the distillers.'

'Pretty bloody, just steaming in circles to make water,' Tim said. 'The lads are fed-up already…'

'The owners — or our people — ought to see this stinking mess,' the old man grumbled. 'Bloody disgrace, this trade…' He left the cabin, muttering darkly.

Tim had already called the hands to stations at 2000, Sunday, 18 August, when the signal from London came through. The situation in Beirut was too dicey: the sheep — or what remained of them — were to be unloaded at Jidda.

The second mate was at the chart table, laying off a fresh course for the fourth time: 'Good grief,' Daniolos said in an aside to Tim. 'I told them to send our mail to Port Said.'

At 2100, *Baitulla* weighed and set course for the port which served Mecca. Though the cool of Suez had been a relief to the humans, the stopping of the engines and the vibration had produced dreadful results in the pens. Sixty-five sheep died on the next day, Monday, 19 August. Then *Baitulla* was in blue water again: no port welcomed this disgusting pollution of their harbours. At sea, the endless string of bloated bodies bothered no one.

The final trial was that Daniolos had no charts with which to enter Jidda harbour. Though Tim had no time for Rittel as a man, the master displayed his seamanship when he sent a boat ahead to sound the passage through the reefs to *Baitulla*'s designated anchorage. At anchor for another day beneath the scorching sun of Jidda Bay, they waited for their berth.

Tempers were raw by the time sunset fell on the festering ship — and sixty-eight sheep died that day. The water around *Baitulla* resounded that night with the sound of macabre splashes.

Dawn broke red and soon it was blistering hot. The cable clanked down the hawse pipe and *Baitulla* was feeling her way across the anchorage to pick up the pilot. At 1120, on Wednesday, 21 August, the ship nudged alongside No. 1 berth. The smells of this teeming port were nothing compared to that welling from the rotting corpses down in the sheep pens.

Tim was standing in the shade beneath the boat deck when Ghazzan came quietly up behind him.

'Sir…'

'Yes?'

'The boys have had enough, sir.'

'What d'you mean?'

'The muck, sir. It's all matted and caked — it'll be hell to shift.'

Tim did not answer at once. 'We'll see about that, bos'n. First, we've got to get this lot ashore. One thousand, three hundred and six sheep less than we loaded … right?'

Ghazzan nodded. 'We've still three days to go yet — they're keeling over like flies down below. And … Mister Mate, sir?'

'Yes, bos'n?'

'Take my warning seriously, sir. The boys…'

'Okay,' Tim said impatiently. 'I'll warn the captain.'

'Sir?' Ghazzan was shifting awkwardly in his sandals. 'I've already told boss, sir.'

Tim felt irritated. Ghazzan and Rittel seemed to be in cahoots. But what the hell — he had only the passage back to Singapore to endure. As he turned towards the bridge, he watched a white-turbaned man, a satchel slung around his shoulders, running — actually running — up the gangway. At the top, he gesticulated with the quartermaster, who pointed in Tim's direction. The man extracted an envelope from his official bag, and began hurrying for'd.

Tim took the telex marked 'Private and Confidential'. The messenger waited for his tip, but Tim had nothing but Australian change. The man departed, cursing and excitedly spreading wide his hands. Tim nipped through the screen door and hurried down to his cabin. He drew the curtains across the doorway. The telex was dated 19 August — last Monday? He tore open the envelope. The message was brief, but surprisingly open:

Both prisoners considered to be alive, but now believed transferred to R.D.'s HQ. C.H.'s life held hostage against release of political prisoners here and in other countries. Fate of fisherman unknown. Regret to inform you that government at this moment are determined not to barter nor to submit to terrorists' threats, nor to other, more audacious, demands.

Strong evidence unknown coup is imminent. Of great assistance to our bargaining position if you can furnish cast-iron proof as soon as possible of our suspicions, as reported to you in my office, Tuesday, 23 July. Do not acknowledge, but destroy. Yong.

Tim re-read the message. He closed his cabin door. He tore up the telex and dropped the shreds into his hand basin. The stink in the ship would more than camouflage the smell of smoke and ashes in his cabin.

CHAPTER FOURTEEN

Even if they had wished to see the sprawling city of Jidda, the crew could not have gone ashore: the stink of the now notorious *Baitulla* was an offence to the city, even above its own flies and choice smells. Four days later, the 23,196 sheep, including the mother and her lamb, had been unloaded. An hour later, the ship was ordered to sail. She could anchor, if she wished, well to seaward, to clean herself. At 1540, on Sunday, 25 August, she let go her anchor, twenty-six days after leaving Fremantle. But for those on board, the stench was almost as objectionable as before. At anchor in this torrid heat, the filth below merely stewed in the sheep pens.

After sunset that evening, Ghazzan reported that over half the crew were refusing to clean out the muck, unless they were guaranteed 'dirty money'. The master took a firm line; the owners and the managers, London Shipping, backed him and the protesting men were paid off. One of the loaded lighters into which the dung was being transferred took the strikers ashore. Local labour was engaged and the ship was soon swarming with gabbling shore gangs.

They started on Monday, beginning in A hold. At the rate at which the gangs worked, the cleaning would take at least five days. The remainder of the crew, sullen and morose, scrubbed and cleaned the wooden decks. And down below men sweated and longed for sea.

By Wednesday, C hold was cleaned up and hosed down. The stench was dying down and morale seemed to Tim to be improving. He was surprised therefore when five more men demanded discharge. They left the ship, and *Baitulla* was now down to a skeleton crew for her passage back to Singapore. On Thursday, the owners came through: when clean, she was to sail to Taiwan where, at a cut price, improvements to the bilge suctions and the sheep water systems were to be undertaken. Even Rittel seemed happier. 'We'll keep "watch on" all the way, so long as we get out of here,' he growled.

D hold was attacked on Thursday, but even the shore gangs were protesting at the working conditions. Shovelling the caked muck into sacks, lugging them along to the hoists, swinging them across on the derricks to the waiting lighters would have been tolerable in cooler weather, but the stink, the flies and the heat made it hell below.

Though the simmering discontent amongst the crew was worrying, Tim's total failure to follow up Yong's allegations was losing him sleep, but on Thursday, during the mid-morning break, came the lead for which he was searching. He left his cabin to find Ghazzan who, during these last two days, had been unobtainable down in the holds with the gangs. Tim, as chief officer, was worried about the manning: any more discharges, and the ship would be compelled to wait in Jidda until more crew could be flown out.

There was no sign of the bos'n, so he would slip down to D hold while it was empty. He could see sufficiently without switching on the lights. The hold smelt sweet and the decks were clean, though the bottom plates were overlapping for the air to circulate until the hold was dry.

Keeping to the shadows, Tim crossed to the far side where the lockers in the bilges were sited. He lifted the lip of a bottom plate and flashed his torch beneath: the locker doors were hanging open and he could smell the red lead. The open padlocks were hanging from the hasps of the fastenings, and the long, rectangular lockers were empty. Fourteen, he counted, and there were probably more beneath the filth in the holds still awaiting cleaning. He snapped out the torch, replaced the plate and silently left the hold.

In the passageway, he ran across three Arab men, their barrows loaded with sacks. They were following a dim figure who was shouting at them to get a move on. Certain that the voice was Ghazzan's, Tim walked quickly for'd to the ladder up to the upper deck. He moved aft to D hold, over which the derricks were plumbed.

The sun was scorching the ship's side. His skin burned as he leaned on the rail to watch the stevedores sheltering in the shade of the lighters' holds during the break. Some were curled in sleep, others were chattering amongst themselves. But Ghazzan was still working the hands during this sacrosanct half-hour break, when he was already having trouble with the gangs...

Tim moved to the lip of the open hold from which the Macgregor covers had been lifted. Standing in the shade at the starboard for'd corner, he peered into the depths three decks below. There, too, men were snatching a few minutes' rest...

The whistles blew and the working parties lethargically drifted back to work: the winches sang, the derricks swung across and down went the whips into the depth of D hold. The empty loading net splurged open upon the floor and was unhooked. A man took the whip across to the other net which was being made up. He was being carefully supervised by three men whom Tim recognized: they were leaning on their empty barrows. In the shadows, Ghazzan stood motionless, watching them.

Tim stepped back from the coaming and hurried across to the other side. He was at the rail when the whip began swinging across towards him. As it began its descent, he stopped the winchman, signalled him to drop the load at his feet. The sudden order upset the operator, who misjudged his distance. The load banged against the rail, then flopped to the deck at Tim's feet.

The knock against the side had split one of the sacks at the bottom of the pile. A white streak in the sack caught Tim's eye. Placing himself between the conical netting and the winchman, he felt into the broken sack. His fingers closed around a packet, soft to his touch. He tweaked it into the scuppers, smothered the damaged sack with one of the others. He stood up, nodded to the operator, and signalled for him to hoist and to load out again into the lighter.

Tim stood on the plastic sachet as he watched the load spiralling down to the lighter. A tall Arab man moved forwards from the gang and, with upstretched arms, guided the net to one side. He waved his mates away, then unhooked the net himself, standing by the sacks as they tumbled out. The hoist whisked upwards, as another load came surging down.

Once again the big fellow took charge, guiding the next load on top of its predecessor. The emptying mound of sacks successfully covered the previous load, and this time there was no doubt of the contents: forty-odd sacks of sheep manure.

Tim picked up the packet at his feet, slipped it inside his shirt. He strode aft to the doorway leading to the officers' quarters. As he stepped inside the screen, he turned. Ghazzan was by the rail, watching him, a smile on his face.

Locking his cabin door, Tim extracted the packet and held it up to the light. Made of strong transparent plastic, it was hermetically sealed across the top — and inside was about a kilogram of a fine white powder. If only Cherry could have been here, she could have confirmed his suspicion — heroin?

A kilogram was worth a fortune...

He sat on the edge of his bunk. Here was the vital proof which Yong needed. He lay back, tucked the packet beneath his pillow and tried to think.

Baitulla was unloading sacks of heroin from underneath the sheep dung. The sheep run was a blind, albeit a profitable cargo. But how was he to get this evidence back to Yong...? And Ghazzan, Tim now sensed, knew that he was holding the incriminating evidence. Tim had the evidence to send him, Ghazzan, and many others in the racket, to jail for life — if not to the executioner. But who were these others in the ship?

Perhaps there had been accomplices amongst those who had just left *Baitulla* — they might have got the wind up. Though the risk of discovery was small, the penalties were formidable: Ghazzan would not risk his neck nor the profits by dealing with more than was absolutely necessary. There was no one else on board who could have organized the plastic packages in the bilge bottoms — or even known about them, because the chief and his boys were flat out keeping their engines and boiler rooms running. No one else...?

And then the incident in the master's cabin flashed into Tim's mind. When he had once entered without waiting for Rittel's 'come in', Ghazzan had been in the act of handing a key back to his captain and Rittel, grabbing it swiftly, had tried to conceal it from Tim. There had been a long silence and then Rittel had changed the subject, dismissing the bos'n summarily — it had been a strained moment, then ... and Ghazzan had once gone to Rittel behind the chief officer's back. Things were adding up. And why did Rittel always wear a chain round his neck, a chain which, in addition to his identity disc, also held a key?

Tim could see it all. Was it entirely an accident that the ship had ended up in Jidda? This port, a city of happy-go-lucky, kind-hearted people, was also the melting pot for the Muslim world. Here, annually, millions of the faithful disembarked on their once-in-a-lifetime pilgrimage to Mecca, only fifty miles away. Through the whirlpool of humanity, every illicit enterprise throve: it was no wonder the authorities had given up trying to halt the drugs — and literally tons were being unloaded from *Baitulla*, straight into Jidda's distribution market. Rittel — and Tim was certain now — was behind this link in the ring. Aircraft were too suspect, but an old, smelly ship…?

Tim climbed from his bunk and opened his bathroom cupboard. He took from the shelf his jumbo tin of colourless foot powder and eased off the top. Then he carefully slit one edge of the heroin sachet. He emptied the drug on to a sheet of paper, then refilled the plastic envelope with talcum. He ditched the remains of the tin down the basin, poured the heroin into the talc tin, and replaced it in the locker. He laid the plastic sachet on the edge of his writing desk, pressing together the edges of the open ends. Then he heated the tip of his penknife blade, tried it on another plastic bag he had in his wardrobe. The material fused. Then he sealed the ends of the heroin packet. He held it to the light, eyeing it from all angles — a passable job.

He leaned across to the internal phone, dialled the bos'n's caboose. Ghazzan was immediately on the line.

'I'd like to see you at once, bos'n.'

'Where, sir?'

'In my office.'

'When?'

110

'Now … and bring the Watch Bill with you, please. We're sailing on Saturday.'

Tim chucked the plastic packet onto his bunk, then sat down at his desk. He extracted the pistol Yong had lent him for the trip, unslipped the safety catch, then carefully replaced it in the drawer, which he left half-open.

CHAPTER FIFTEEN

At the end of each interminable day, as soon as Cherry felt the first cool of evening, she scratched another nick in the bamboo lintel of her banana-leaved hut. The days were drawing in, for she counted forty-nine days (could it be only seven weeks?) since that night on the island when she had so nearly regained her liberty. Seven weeks… She shuddered, holding her grubby rags about her, the same dress she had been wearing on the morning of their capture.

'Miss Cherry…'

This pretence at polite behaviour nauseated her. She got up and followed the guard who was waiting for her outside, his eyes arrogantly undressing her. She couldn't care less, for she'd been through all the degradation already. The other soldier locked up behind her, and then she began her ritual walk to the summit of this islet to which she could give no name. If it had not been so small, the thick woods through which the path curled could have been called a jungle, the vegetation was so lush and thick. Her feet were hard now after her sandals had disintegrated, but during the first few weeks this climb had been one of the lesser trials in her identical days.

The light through the leaves ahead was showing at last — and then, shoved brutally from behind, Cherry floundered into the small clearing on the summit of the island. They left her there, as on every evening, alone, with only the soldier lookout in the tree, thirty yards away, but able to watch her. She fell to the ground, weak with lack of food and exercise, and tried to regain her breath.

She never knew how long she would be allowed this interlude, a strange privilege accorded her by Tumelaka. She never knew whether he would come up here, a habit he had given up only last week. But after the horror of those first terrible days before she had been taken to this island for exchange, Tumelaka had been at pains to demonstrate the ruthlessness of the discipline he enforced on his terrorists … and she closed her eyes to shut out the memory of those nightmare days.

On the third evening in her hut, still not recovered from the shock of her kidnapping, her guard had been increased to three men, all in the same uniform of sloppy jungle-green trousers, tucked into soft-soled boots, green sweatshirts and jungle peaked caps. But on this evening, they were whispering outside the flimsy door. Through the crack, she recognized that Malay skipper who had been captured with her. His face was puffed and his eyes half-closed from a beating-up, and he was dressed like the other two. Her evening food was normally brought in by one soldier, but this time two came in, one with the bowl of 'soup' and a chunk of mouldy rice bread.

The offering was shoved towards her by the first man, a small soldier of about eighteen. They stood back, eyeing her in silence as she gulped down the soup, watching them above the lip of the bowl. Before she had finished, the tall man crept silently round the edge of the hut, his teeth white as he grinned at her from the gloom. She stood still, her head following him, her whole being tense as she recognized the gleam in the man's eyes. Suddenly she was grabbed from behind by the smaller soldier, who knocked the bowl from her hand. He clamped his hand across her mouth, then dragged her backwards into the darkest corner away from the door. The next moments would remain with her for the rest of her life.

The youth at her back straddled her, his knees thrusting into the hollows of her shoulder sockets, his free hand holding her left arm. She struggled frenziedly, wriggling and kicking as, in the darkness, she watched dumbly while the larger man stood over her. She could hear his breathing, that was all ... and those wild eyes of his as he flopped down upon her. She felt his hands upon her and then, with all her strength, her fingers tore at the hand muzzling her mouth. Her teeth sank into the small soldier's palm. She tasted blood and, as he recoiled in pain, she screamed...

She remembered the shaft of light as the door was flung open. She heard the crash of splintering wood, the grunts of struggling men — and then a shot outside. The weight of her attacker suddenly lifted and then she heard shouts and running footsteps. Jaafar Hamzah, the Malay man, was crouched by the doorway, spitting blood, as a group of soldiers surrounded the hut. She recognized their leader as the thickset sergeant, the murderers who had executed the schooner's crew — and then, seconds later, Tumelaka, a drawn pistol in his hand, loped into the clearing.

Later that night, by the light of the flickering torches, she had been forced to watch the two soldiers pay for their indiscipline. They were each tied to a stake. Each one was naked, their limbs splayed apart... She could still hear the screams, then the two shots which put an end to their agony.

Cherry opened her eyes, still not completely certain that the episode had not been a nightmare ... but the memory recurred, each night in the early hours. When she next saw Tumelaka, it had been up here, in this summit clearing. And it had been a strange meeting, disclosing a new side of the man that did not add up. He seemed deranged.

Two weeks afterwards, she saw Hamzah again. He bore a chevron on his arm and seemed to be in charge of a small section. He had averted his eyes from her, but he was meting it out good and strong to his men, who seemed not to resent his severity. That was the evening when Tumelaka had joined her up here. It had been a strange meeting: with intense pride, like Satan outside Jerusalem, he had boasted of his kingdom, sweeping his arms towards Sumatra.

'Do you see there, Miss Hok? That's Mount Surangan, the highest peak in the Asahan range. From there to the northern coast of Sumatra, my army controls everything that happens. The people support me, waiting for the day of revolution. I protect them from the injustices of their present masters, whose regime is rotten with corruption. As soon as we receive our full quota of arms, we'll take over.'

Tumelaka's eyes were shining, his face twitching with frightening intensity. 'With our brothers in Southeast Asia, in Japan, in the Philippines, we'll sweep society clean of capitalism. Then we'll have a free world, run by the workers in their millions. You'll see, Miss Hok.' He looked down briefly at Cherry, touched her head. 'And you're a pawn in our plans, Miss Hok, a very valuable pawn. While you're alive, you're useful to us. But if anything were to go wrong with our present demands…' His face shivered, as if a cloud were passing over. The eyes glaring down at her were insane.

'I'll have you for myself. Until then, I've promised Singapore and the boss that you won't be harmed. They'll hang our two freedom fighters who are under suspended death sentence in Changi, if you're returned … harmed.' Then Tumelaka had swaggered into the undergrowth, leaving Cherry alone in this clearing. And that was almost three weeks ago, while she supposed negotiations were continuing — her life the forfeit.

Cherry felt chilled by the contrast of dusk after the sweltering, humid hut. She curled her arms about her filthy dress, walked briskly back and forth across the clearing. This was the moment when she always counted the light flashes sweeping across the leafy filigrees to the north. They must be the beams from a lighthouse — flashes about every five seconds, perhaps a little longer.

This hidden headquarters must be concealed on an island, because sometimes she could hear the roar of breaking surf, the calling of seabirds; and, when the wind was right, she was sure she could hear the thrumming of boat engines — she had certainly been brought here by sea the night they had escaped from the ransom rendezvous…

During the past few days, Cherry had noted a gradual intensifying of activity. Her rations had been brought to her more irregularly — once, when she could stand the hunger no longer and had cried out, the Malay skipper had sauntered into the hut with a minion carrying her rice and rotting mangoes. By his treachery and toadying, he had evidently raised himself to the middle-ranks of Tumelaka's men. Hamzah had laughed contemptuously when he'd left the hut, taking the fruit with him, and shouting arrogantly at the other guard.

She heard the swish of parting foliage. Tumelaka was standing at the top of the path, eyeing her inquisitively. Tonight he was dressed in full battle dress, as he had been on the ransom night. His jungle green was belted tight and a gun was slung on one hip.

'You've got five minutes to get yourself ready,' he snapped.

'Where're you taking me?'

'To sea. I've got a lot to do.' His eyes were gleaming, his face fanatical. 'We've been waiting a long time for tonight.'

'Who's "we"?' Cherry asked boldly as she walked towards the path.

'The Red Dragons,' he said softly. 'I've already told you: I'm leader of their Sumatran command.' His face clamped tight. He grabbed her arm as she was trying to pass him. He wrenched her against him, his arms steel bands about her. He held her without speaking, motionless beneath the darkening tunnel of jungle. He pulled at the back of her hair, forcing her to look into his face.

He was gazing down at her, his eyes flickering with lust, his wide lips compressed. Cherry tried to slide from his grasp, but he held her rigidly. She could hear his breathing, feel the pumping of his heart against her breast. She fought against him, but his arms were crushing her until she cried out. But still he stood rigid, pressing himself to her. She could see his teeth gleaming in the gloom as he grinned down at her. She jerked up her knee. He grunted, pushed her from him, then grabbed at her wrist.

'Follow me,' he hissed. 'You're coming in my boat.'

Tumelaka began loping down the path. The leafy tendrils flicked Cherry's face as she scrambled after him, trying to keep up.

'Number 5 clear of the reef…' the loudspeaker crackled.

Tumelaka reached for the R/T mic on the side of the bridge. 'Roger,' he acknowledged. 'Leaving harbour now.'

He nodded to the cox'n in the armoured wheelhouse at his feet. 'Take her out, cox'n. Slow ahead both engines.'

He was relieved to be putting to sea. The tension and last-minute preparations of the past few days had left him drained.

Organizing his clandestine flotilla demanded forethought: fetching the stores, ammunition and fuel from across the water, ready on the wharf at Teluk Nibung, halfway up the Asahan estuary. Though he flew the navy's ensign during the day (the authorities turned a blind eye to their forces' piracy activities) it was simple continuing with his own affairs at night. Jakarta did not want to know… None of his ships wore ensigns at night, showed no lights … and as his boat, Number 1, eased through the reef, he saw the darkened silhouette spread out to the nor'eastward, wallowing gently in the swell. He took a fleeting look astern, at the dark outline of the wooded island that was his base.

Salahnama was the ideal hideout. Between the two shipping routes to Penang, from Tiram and Napal, no one approached its dangerous reefs too closely. Pandang and its rocky lighthouse was a bastion to the north, while the foul water to the east was a deterrent. Inquisitive fishermen had been appropriately warned off, not a difficult exercise, with his forces extracting their 'protection' funds from all the villages in the hinterland. He glanced at the waves breaking around the base of the rock passing down his starboard side.

'Half ahead together,' he commanded. He felt the surge of power, gripped the rail as the acceleration jerked him backwards. He groped for the R/T: 'Form on leader,' he ordered. 'Formation One.'

Tumelaka had trained his flotilla to a satisfactory efficiency. Each commanding officer had done the course in Leningrad before these P4s had been bought from the North Koreans. Now that the torpedo tubes had been replaced by the 25-mm gun mountings, these fast attack craft were ideal in these waters. The conversion had cost only a couple of knots — they could still knock up forty-eight knots in sea conditions like tonight's.

'Course 120. Two-five revolutions, cox'n.'

The farthest boats were already swinging out on either quarter, their silhouettes low as they dug in their sterns. Pandang's flashes were gleaming to the north, the reflection of the beam shining brightly on the calm sea. He had left only a skeleton party on the island base to man communications with Red Dragon; the bossman was already at sea somewhere off South Vietnam. It had taken time to perfect the vital requirement of communication: without the Russians, he would never have solved that one. The satellite aerial dome was concealed near the summit on Salahnama. The chopper boys from Senebui had even been unable to detect the UHF aerials amongst the trees.

'Course, sir, 120…' His cox'n was a first-class man. Reliable and ruthless, he was a fanatical member of the team. Tumelaka had found him, by accident, up in the north, rather as he had stumbled across Hamzah. He, too, could make officer grade in the Dragons. Tumelaka glanced astern.

His last boat, Number 4, was swinging into station… Four bow-waves, their phosphorescence gleaming in the darkness, the thrum-thrum of the diesel engines; the wind buffeting his face: his spirit lifted and he felt exhilarated. Another few minutes and he would turn them to the southward, to One Fathom Bank and their allotted areas.

Tumelaka's orders from the boss were succinct: the Dragons were short of funds again. There would be blatant piracy — quite simple-until 0100. The boys enjoyed that. During the early hours they would begin preparing for the big thing, Operation Red Justice, timed for tomorrow night.

During the daylight hours of the following day, his five boats would disperse to act independently, quietly patrolling inside territorial waters in their official roles, upholding law and order under the aegis of the Indonesian ensign. The crews could catch up on sleep for the hard night ahead… The commanding officers would be briefing their crews on Operation Red Justice during the afternoon tomorrow. Tonight, until 0100, would be 'fun for the boys'…

Until 0100, each boat had her orders, each to her own sector, to attack any worthwhile target — and that meant saleable goods, not women, as he had sternly reminded the ships' companies. Number 4, commanded by Kyai, the young Papuan man, who was intent on outdoing the others in ruthlessness, had been allotted the Durian Strait; 5, Long Bank off Rangsang; 3, off Medan; 2, the approaches to the Dumai Strait, amongst the shoals off Rupat.

For himself, he had the area with the richest potential — One Fathom Bank. Tumelaka would stay inside the Aruah islands and nip out for a likely target…

The rest of the night, from 0100 until dawn, would be hard work: completing half the tasks set by the boss in preparation for zero hour at 2000 tomorrow night. Tumelaka had given his COs precise written orders for this first part of the operation: Number 4 would start taking out the Decca chain along the southern shore of the Malay coast; he would finish the job tomorrow night. Number 2 would extinguish the buoys and the new beacon north of One Fathom Bank; he would shoot up and extinguish Jemur light on the Aruah islands tomorrow night. Number 5 would cause havoc down south, moving, sinking and extinguishing the buoys; he would take out the Decca chain on the Indonesian side tomorrow.

Number 3 and he, Tumelaka, in Number 1, were to extinguish the new flashing beacon at the southern end of the southeast lane on One Fathom Bank. They would then lay the decoy with its reflector (it was stowed aft at the moment) three miles south, on the extremity of the dumping ground patch, in eighteen metres of water. Tomorrow, at dusk, Number 1 and Number 3 would shoot up One Fathom Bank lighthouse and destroy its communications.

Tumelaka glanced at his watch: nearly 2015 already, and dark as pitch. Number 4 had a long way to go. He must release his marauders… He reached for the mic.

'Proceed as ordered,' he snapped. 'Stand by…'

Each boat came up, a curt acknowledgement, just as he had trained them — no unnecessary chatter.

'*Execute*…'

Tumelaka turned to watch the attack craft breaking off, their washes foaming in the darkness as they surged to full speed. Swiftly they merged with the horizon, vanished into the night.

'Port ten. Steer for Jemur light.' He pulled back the bridge throttles.

The wind fanned his face softly as she fell off the chine and ploughed slowly towards the Aruah islands. His concentration was disturbed by his insistent craving for the woman in his cabin below.

'Cox'n…'

'Sir?'

'The hands can relax for half an hour. Action stations at 2100. We'll knock out the northwest beacon first.'

'Aye, aye, sir.'

'And Cox'n…'

'Sir?'

'Come up and take over. Steer for Jemur light. I'm going down below.'

'Right, sir...'

Tumelaka turned over the boat and hurried from the bridge. He, too, had half an hour — more than enough time alone with the woman — before the night's carnage began.

CHAPTER SIXTEEN

'She's all yours, then,' Stefan Daniolos said, handing over his watch. 'Can't you see the new beacon yet? That's the loom of One Fathom Bank. I've told the Old Man.'

Tim watched the second mate pushing wearily against the after bridge door. Stefan and he had been watch on, watch off for eleven days now, since leaving the Jidda anchorage. The other officers had quit, but Rittel was determined to sail, even with such a skeleton crew, and for once Tim had supported him. Tim moved to the steering repeater, checked the course with the helmsman, then stuck his face into the ancient radar's visor. Several ships ahead, all safe ... and the Aruah islands coming up fine on the starboard bow.

He glanced up and saw the loom of One Fathom Bank light ahead on the horizon; but where was the newly established beacon guarding the north-western extremity of the northwest bound lane in the separation zone? He pored over the chart, took a Decca fix. They'd be entering the southeast lane in twenty minutes. Navigation marks were notoriously chaotic in this area: buoys out of position, lights not reported as extinguished until days afterwards — and even the Admiralty chart, 1353, ran out through the middle of the trickiest section of One Fathom Bank. Daniolos had forgotten to provide 3946 — the full-scale of the bank — and Tim fumbled into the chart table drawer...

He spread out the chart, began transferring his Decca fix which did not make sense — at least he could check his position with the loom of One Fathom Bank and Jemur on the Aruah islands, broad now on his starboard beam. He moved out to his starboard wing to take another bearing of Jemur. He crouched over the azimuth ring — one flash every five seconds — 232° — just in time, for menacing black clouds were swirling up from the westward. It was his bad luck to encounter one of these Sumatran rain squalls at the entrance to the separation zone. Things had changed again, Daniolos had moaned (the flashing starboard-hand buoy was still missing from its station, apparently), but no one had had the time to wade through the mountains of navigational bumph — in itself incomplete — which they had picked up at Fremantle. The rest of the stuff was probably awaiting them in Port Said with the mail they had missed.

Most seafarers exercised their own discretion here — even the countries bordering the Strait could not agree amongst themselves, though Tim had heard that, at the last conference, the United Nations were operating some sort of surveillance and anti-piracy patrol. He moved back into the wheelhouse and slapped the bearings on the new chart. Then he went to the bridge window, saw the new separation zone buoy flashing further to starboard than he had expected, and watched One Fathom light drifting into focus as the storm clouds rushed up from the starboard beam. He must rouse Rittel if the squall didn't pass astern.

Eleven days ... nearly twelve now, the time ten minutes past midnight of this Thursday, 12 September. *Baitulla* was still making seventeen knots, but the chief was at his wits' end with condenseritis in the feed water. Twice during the eight-till-four he had had to shut down one boiler ... but, lurking behind Tim's fatigue and the drag of alternate watches, it was the sinister atmosphere which was really getting him down. He carried Yong's pistol with him all the time now, even in his bunk. He was convinced that Ghazzan had run straight to

Rittel, as soon as Tim had finished with the bos'n on that last Thursday in Jidda.

Ghazzan had acted 'wet', claiming no knowledge of the split sack and its contents. Tim had said nothing when he'd showed the sachet to Ghazzan in his cabin — he merely showed the bos'n the thing, then took it up top, where he slung it over the side. No comment, no further reference did anyone make to the incident until Rittel spoke to Tim one forenoon, about the sixth day out. Alone in the wings of the bridge, he deviously came round to the affair, probing, trying to read Tim's mind. 'Of course, Simkins,' he murmured, staring down at the lifeboat beneath him, 'if you'd found something incriminating, you'd probably report it, wouldn't you?'

'Incriminating?'

'Forget it.' Rittel had shrugged his shoulders and stomped off below. And there was the evening when, coming down from the four-to-eight, Tim was sure someone had been through his cabin. Yet the talc tin did seem untouched...

The steaming lights of a ship were coming up on his port bow, westward bound, the bearing just altering. She should pass well clear, so long as she was properly inside her northwest lane — and there was a faint light showing intermittently ahead. Someone ahead, whom *Baitulla* was overtaking... Tim was moving across to the radar when he sensed someone behind him. He turned, saw Rittel's bulk approaching.

'What's going on, Mister Mate? Why haven't you called me?'

'I was...'

The master was lumbering out to the starboard wing and Tim followed. As he stood behind Rittel, who was crouched over the bearing ring, a shadow detached itself from behind the bridge screen.

Rittel straightened, confronting Tim. 'We don't believe you, Simkins,' he said softly, out of the helmsman's hearing. 'Grab him, Ghazzan.'

A slight figure pounced forwards. As Tim glimpsed the glint of steel, he jerked backwards, his back to the screen. He reached for his gun under his shirt.

'We're not taking any further risks with you, Simkins,' Rittel rasped. 'The tides and the fish'll take care of you.' Before Tim could act, he was peering into the snout of an ugly automatic. At the same moment, he felt the speed coming off the ship. The engine-room phone was ringing from the wheelhouse.

'Watch him, Ghazzan,' Rittel snapped. 'I'll deal with the ship.' He slid through the door, grabbed the phone. Tim slowly withdrew his empty hand and stood poised to counter Ghazzan's knife thrust. They stood facing each other in the darkness, Ghazzan's face split with an evil smile.

Things moved fast then, as Ghazzan, watching his adversary like a snake, spotted something sliding down the starboard side. Tim saw it too, a low, sleek hull, darkened and turning rapidly towards… Seconds later, there was the sharp rattle of small arms fire from astern. Orange flashes flickered about the poop deck and then there was the sound of men's voices, yelling and screaming from somewhere aft in the ship.

Ghazzan leaped to the rail and leant over the side. '*Pirates…*' he yelled. 'There's a boat alongside, captain.' There was a whistling sound and then Ghazzan fell, his head shattered by an explosive bullet. His small body flopped to the deck, the fingers of his hands still twitching on the haft of his knife. Crouching low, Tim rushed into the wheelhouse. The opposite door flung open and a mob of masked men, in commando-type dress, surged through the opening. Rittel stood and faced them, blazing away with his automatic until he was scythed in half by an automatic pistol.

The helmsman had scurried from the wheel at the first cry of alarm. They found him cowering in the corner, then put a bullet through his head, as Tim grabbed the wheel. He felt the cold barrel of a gun against the back of his head, as a tall man snapped in good English: 'Take her through the channel…'

Tim heard the snick of a safety catch being released as he struggled to check the ship's swing to port. As he spun the spokes, a man was yelling from the doorway. Tim looked up, through the windows. A green light, with two white lights above it, was very close — and then he glimpsed the loom of a ship's bows as torrential rain began slashing against the wheelhouse roof. There was a flash of lightning and then the screaming of the wind as the squall hit them. It was suddenly as black as pitch, and even the lights of the approaching ship had vanished.

CHAPTER SEVENTEEN

Normally, Captain Thostrop was unruffled by the vicissitudes of his professional calling, having for all his adult life been at sea, helping to deliver the world's goods. Peder Thostrop was a competent master, proud of his RO/RO ship, MV *Svensborj*, which had been designed specifically with side-opening doors for the car trade between Nagasaki and Liverpool. Tonight, he had begun his approach to the separation zone of One Fathom Bank with misgivings. Though he was fully loaded with Japanese cars, his 21,000-ton ship would still have water to spare under her keel, even over the shallowest patches. But, as he had instructed his second mate, he would take *Svensborj* well to the southward of the northwest lane, as close to the separation line as he dared, to give the Amazon Maru Shoal as much clearance as possible.

He had not been able to find the green quick-flashing buoy marking the new wreck to the northwest of Pyramid Shoal; and since then, things had not been adding up satisfactorily. None of his Decca fixes were reliable, due probably to local atmospheric conditions — that black horizon to the westward boded no good, and visibility was definitely shutting down. Mercifully, though he was sighting One Fathom Bank light only intermittently, his officer of the watch had sighted the flashing beacon marking the south-eastern end of the southeast lane. Curiously, though a light was now clearly visible, the echo was a feeble blip on the radar screen — and then he saw a ship steaming south in the other lane, about four and a half miles distant.

'What's the bearing of the beacon, then?'

'265°. I'm just putting it on, sir.'

Thostrop waited impatiently for the two-point fix, the last on One Fathom light bringing him nicely into the north-westerly lane. The navigator glanced upwards at the clock: 0029.

'Good God, man, we're almost on Amazon Bank.' He glanced at the echo sounder: still twenty-eight fathoms.

'Hard-a-port,' he rapped. He knocked back the revs to twenty-two knots. He moved swiftly back to the chart table, laid off a bold alteration to the westward. 'Steer 268°,' he rapped. 'Steering in hand.'

The officer of the watch had at last sensed the urgency of the moment. The helmsman jumped to the small steering handle.

Peder Thostrop felt the warning bells inside himself. His instinct had never let him down yet. He pricked off two miles along the new course. How long at twenty-two knots…?

'Alter back to 315° in six minutes,' he ordered. 'This'll take us safely clear. We'll be right on the southern edge of our lane.'

'Aye, aye, sir.' The second mate was peering through his binoculars. 'Ship crossing from port to starboard, sir. I can see her steaming lights … and her green's showing.'

The master dodged into the radar visor. 'Two and a half miles,' he murmured. 'What the devil's she doing there?'

'A rogue, sir, probably,' the second said. 'Could be one of the Medan to Malacca ferries…'

Thostrop snatched at the officer's glasses. 'She's turning, second … *turning back to starboard.*' He kept the binoculars glued on the madman. The steaming lights were fining up, were crossing, and now her red was gleaming.

At that moment, the second shouted, 'Six minutes, sir. Shall I come back to starboard?'

'I've got the ship,' the captain snapped. He was crouched over the pelorus, checking the bearing. 'She's steady,' he muttered. 'Hard-a-port, stop both engines.' He snapped at the officer of the watch: 'Sound two short blasts.' His heart was in his mouth while he waited interminably for *Svensborj* to start her swing. Suddenly, a screaming wind hit them and then down fell the rain in curtains of water that only a tropical squall could produce. A blast of wind clattered against the bridge windows. The night was blotted out. The approaching ship vanished. The *Svensborj*'s siren boomed twice above them.

'Ease the wheel...' Thostrop glanced at the heading. 'Starboard fifteen — steer 190°.' He would be crossing into the other lane, but he could not risk a full circle, in case the madman had altered back. There had been no sound signal from her... The clock showed 0037, three minutes since wheel-over. Speed was coming off, down to twelve knots, but he must bring her back or he'd be right in the thick of the other lane...

He pushed the siren button himself: four shorts — a pause — another short boomed above the fury of the squall.

'Starboard twenty. Keep your eyes skinned, second.'

But the binoculars never reached Captain Thostrop's eyes. The ship juddered suddenly, lurched crazily to port. He was hurled to the deck and lay, half dazed, watching the log falling back ... eight ... seven ... five knots.

He grabbed at the bridge rail, hauled himself to his feet, balancing against the list that was already developing. He felt the explosions from somewhere deep in the ship as bulkheads collapsed, and then he heard the scream of tortured metal. Suddenly she was taking on a bow-down angle. He held himself upright by the rail and peered through the bridge windows. Water was already sweeping down the fo'c'sle head, a torrent of dark water, then a deluge of foaming sea.

He jumped for the alarm bell button, yelled at the top of his voice: '*Abandon ship...*' He heard the distant ringing of the alarm bells — and then the lights snapped out. In the total darkness, he began hauling himself towards the screen door, following the second who was waiting there, his hand outstretched to help.

'I've switched on the Mayday,' the young man gasped. 'I've taken a look at the chart, sir. I've no idea...'

'We've hit an underwater obstruction,' Thostrop shouted. He was shaking his head, talking to himself. 'I don't understand,' he was muttering. 'God, I don't understand...'

They were the last words he spoke. His body, with twenty-six others, went down with the ship. She plummeted to the bottom, in thirty-one metres of water, taking her load of cars, twenty-six men and the master's wife with her. There was only one survivor, the ship's second officer. At dawn, the Kelang lifeboat picked him up, only six cables from the dangerous wreck reported in 1972.

CHAPTER EIGHTEEN

Tim knew, during the carnage taking place in the darkness about him, the elemental terror that compels self-preservation. But in the surge of panic mounting inside him, only one instinct called him — the safety of his ship. And as he gripped the slippery spokes, running with the blood of the dying helmsman being hacked to pieces in the corner, he desperately forced his mind to think calmly. Nothing else mattered. The tall man directing operations had spotted the lights of the advancing ship, heard her siren booming so close in the darkness... She could be only cables away, plunging through this squall which was blacking out the night.

The approaching ship had turned away to port. Tim had distinctly counted her two blasts ... and *Baitulla* was still swinging to starboard, in spite of his frenzied 'hard-over', trying to meet her. And then above the pandemonium he heard the siren booming again in the night. He counted them — four shorts, a pause, then another short. She was manoeuvring to starboard again. He lunged for the engine telegraphs and shoved them to full ahead.

He must cross the lane, get out of this as soon as he could. He'd have to take the risk. Perhaps someone was still alive in the engine room. He spun back the wheel to starboard as the tall pirate sprang towards him, watching his every movement.

'You know what you're doing, Englishman?' the swine shouted in English. 'Where's the other ship?'

Tim, wrestling with the steering, ignored him, his eyes glued to the swinging compass card... 210° ... 215° ... 218°. He spun back the wheel and eased to meet her. He was settling on

225° when the radio began crackling loudly from the starboard screen: '*Mayday... Mayday... Mayday...* This is Motorship *Svensborj* sinking in position south of One Fathom...'

The message died.

The tall man, whom Tim now recognized suddenly as the odious pirate who had captured the schooner, wrenched at the wheel. Tim was grabbed from behind and flung against the after bulkhead. A couple of faces grinned at him, their eyes crazed, knives in their fists. One of them drew his gun and pressed the muzzle against Tim's temple. He closed his eyes. He knew no fear now, only relief that the horror was ending ... and Cherry's smiling face swam before him; her hands stretched out to him, her fingers trying to caress his face...

Suddenly, Tim was knocked sideways. As he fell he glimpsed another thug, an automatic pistol in his hands. He had knocked the gun from the other man's grasp and kicked it into the gloom. The face peering into his was a grim Malay face, somehow familiar... For an instant recognition flickered... Then the man was screaming at the two maniacs trying to keep their feet on the slippery deck, as the ship heeled wildly to starboard.

'Against the chart table...' the Malay man barked. Tim winced as the automatic prodded him in the guts. As he stumbled towards the space, the ship lurched, quivering throughout her length. Her bows began rearing into the night and then everyone was slithering to the deck. In the pandemonium, her safety valves lifted, the roar of the escaping steam shattering the night.

The hands were still visible on the face of the clock which hung on the for'd screen above the wheel: from the light of his torch, Tumelaka watched the second hand flicking across the dial. It was already 0053, and he still had a lot to do before dawn. Things were almost out of control: his prize had run hard aground on some bank to the southward, and his men had run amok, forgetting their prime duty to loot valuables. By the feel of her, the ship was stuck here. Someone had already yelled from below that she was making water rapidly. The captain was dead. He caught sight of Simkins and went over to him.

'Show me where we are aground.' Tumelaka encouraged the bearded man with a clout across the face. 'Show me on the chart...' He followed the prisoner's finger. 'As I thought — southeast of the dumping ground.' He turned to his man with the automatic. 'Hamzah, signal Number 1 alongside. We've wasted too much time...' A man stumbled through the doorway and passed a message to his commander. Hamzah hustled to the doorway, then began flashing his lamp.

By the light of his own torch, Tumelaka rapidly read the top priority signal. It was from the boss, his orders firm and unambiguous, as usual. Operation Red Justice was advanced twenty-four hours, due to *Shoysa Maru*'s sailing a day early from Lutong, Shell's terminal in Borneo. Clearance had been obtained from Singapore and she would be passing through Singapore's Main Strait at dawn. She was in ballast, drawing fourteen metres and would be passing through at twelve knots, ETA St John island, just before high water at 0450 today, Thursday.

Tumelaka stood motionless, allowing the coming and going to continue unheeded. Fortunately, failing to find any worthwhile prizes, he had carried out his deception tasks, but he and the others now had only five hours to take out the Decca chains; and to interfere with the communications, including the jamming, both of R/T and navigational aids.

But they were all ready, if he passed his executive orders immediately to his COs. He himself, in Number 1, was close to One Fathom Bank lighthouse. He could knock it out and still have time to land at Pelampong for the attack. But, with this emergency on his hands, he could not be certain that all would be complete … and he could not pass this information over the air, for security reasons, to the Eastern Commando waiting on Pelampong. If he could not warn them, the assault troops might not be ready or the whole operation would collapse due to false assumptions.

'Number 1's alongside the port quarter, commander.'

It was Hamzah, who hated the enemy with a fanaticism that startled even Tumelaka, sometimes.

'Where's the Englishman?'

'In the boat, sir. He's locked below.'

'Take the inflatable and land him on Senebui island. You know these waters. There'll be a chopper waiting for you. You've got to be at Advanced Base on Pelampong by 0430 — understand?'

'What about my squad, sir? They're in the first wave.'

Tumelaka was attempting to write the message for the Advanced Base CO. He looked up impatiently. 'I'll bring them with me,' he rapped. 'Don't worry, I'll be there — we've got forty-eight knots. Here, give this to the Pelampong commanding officer.' He folded the paper. 'Don't let the prisoner escape, Hamzah. We'll be needing him.'

Hamzah was gazing at him, his black eyebrows raised.

'Show him the woman before you shove off,' Tumelaka ordered. 'Now, get going... She's in the cabin, d'ye understand?'

Hamzah nodded, turned smartly and disappeared aft into the darkness.

Tumelaka followed and yelled for his top sergeant. 'Kill anyone left alive,' he shouted. 'Don't forget the engine room.'

As he clambered on board Fast Attack Craft Number 1, he heard the shots from below and the sound of running footsteps as the rearguard ran aft, their work done. He waited for them to clamber over the boat's guardrail. He glanced across his stern, and saw that the inflatable was clear and that the two occupants were in it.

'Bear off for'd,' he shouted. 'Slow ahead, Cox'n. Steer for One Fathom Bank lighthouse.'

Jaafar Hamzah opened the throttle of the twin-engined inflatable. The squall was passing clear astern, and the wind was good in his face as the boat bounced at full speed across the sea, which was swiftly resuming its placid calm. He held on to a lanyard with his left hand, signalled to the Englishman to stay low, crouching on the bottom boards. Though he knew these waters blindfolded, he had to keep his eyes skinned, for there might be floating debris about tonight. He would keep to the westward to avoid the drying patches of South Sands.

It would be difficult picking up the low-lying country, but he would find Senebui Point, then double back for the eastern tip of the island: the coast was steep — to where the helicopter strip had been cleared in the scrub. It was good to be away, the wind in his face and the Englishman the only man with him. Simkins turned towards him, yelling above the roar of the engines and the slap-slapping of the boat.

'She didn't know me, Jaafar. She didn't speak.'

Hamzah shook his head. 'She couldn't see you properly. It was only for a second.' He eased the inflatable off to starboard: the breakers were showing white on South Sands. 'We'll talk later,' he shouted. 'Don't give up hope for her, Mr Simkins. She's still alive, isn't she?'

Another half hour ... on the last few miles, he tossed a spare grenade into the bottom boards. He tapped the butt of his automatic slung about his chest. 'I'm all right,' he yelled.

Then the point came up, the low outline of Senebui island dark against the land. It slid past a mile and a half off, until the point came abeam. Jaafar throttled back and turned sharply to starboard, the point dead ahead.

'Keep silence,' he muttered. 'They'll be watching us.'

Three cables from the silver strand of surf, he turned again to starboard. The separating creek, still dry at half-tide, slipped slowly down his port side. When only a hundred metres off, he sighted the hard.

'Get ready to jump,' he murmured above the coughing of the outboards. 'We hate each other — don't forget that.' He cut the motors, felt her scraping the hard. 'Jump!' he shouted, pointing his gun at Simkins's stomach. 'Try anything and I'll shoot.'

Jaafar secured the painter, then prodded his prisoner up the ramp. They reached an opening in the scrub, and several shadows formed behind them, silent, guns in their hands. Ten minutes later, the scrub opened before them to show the dim outlines of four helicopters, one with its rotors revolving, its crew-member waiting by the door. They prodded their prisoner into the machine, slapping a helmet on him as the motors' whine increased. Five minutes later, the pre-checks done, the rotors swirling, she lifted off, canted to starboard then lunged forwards to the southeast.

The crewman, crouching in the darkness as he elbowed his way aft to them, shouted into Jaafar's ear: '*Pisang mas...*' He shoved the small bananas into Jaafar's hands. 'He'll be needing some too... It's two hours to the island.'

Jaafar nodded. Simkins would be needing food before this day was done.

CHAPTER NINETEEN

Tim was jolted from his doze by the swoop of the chopper towards the string of islands, to the left of the red and white flashes from the lighthouse. That must be Pulau Takong Kechil, with Takong Besar coming up underneath them now… The machine flew on, up to the northwest, then, to Tim's surprise, swept past the islet of Pelampong. He watched the islet sliding astern and then the chopper was hovering over what looked like the deck of a land-borne aircraft-carrier — a long, narrow islet with a few trees on it, a sandy beach on its eastern side, deeper water to the west.

Jaafar pushed him out when the chopper touched, and then they were escorted towards a sleek craft rolling gently in the calm. A dory pulled them out and, as he clambered up the jumping ladder, he recognized her as similar to the fast attack craft which had attacked *Baitulla*. But this was Number 5 and the short man glaring down from her bridge was not Tumelaka, although her armament seemed the same, bristling with twin mountings, boarding ramps and grapnels.

Jaafar held Tim by the neck, kept him aft amidships, abreast the starboard mounting, as the boat nudged slowly astern. When she reached deep water, she moved slowly ahead on one engine; she threaded her way through a cluster of drying islets, then crept in under the lee of what must be Pelampong. A similar FAC, with the number 4 painted on her bows, was lying off.

'She's ours,' Jaafar whispered. 'Kyai's boat, taking the first wave.' He raised his voice: 'Jump, you bastard. You'll have to get your feet wet.'

Tim was shoved from behind and floundered ashore, watched by the guffawing crew. Soldiers emerged from a group of huts, grabbed him roughly and bound him to a tree. He watched Jaafar, striding importantly across the clearing, salute someone who was observing the scene. He handed something to the officer who then began barking orders.

Men scurried from the huts, carrying their weapons, stacking them in five piles upon the beach. They had barely finished when he heard a throaty purr from seaward, the sound of an approaching FAC. He craned his neck to watch the low silhouettes creeping into the lee of the island: Numbers 1 and 3.

The leading boat gave a kick astern to stop close to the beach. They shouldered Tumelaka ashore and he strutted across the clearing to meet the island's boss. Tim watched them, a chart on the ground, hands gesticulating, pricking off distances. Finally they checked their watches: 0445. Tim heard the low thrum of another boat close behind him. In silence, the weapons were loaded into the boats.

Jaafar swaggered up to him and sliced at his bonds. Jabbing him in the back, he prodded him towards Number 4. 'Kyai's dangerous,' he whispered. 'Stick with me — whatever happens.' He struck Tim across the face, laughing softly. Floundering through the water, they clambered on board the wallowing boat.

Jaafar took Tim aft and tied him to a rail by one of the smoke floats. Then he disappeared for'd. Tim felt the jerk as she went ahead, watched the vapour floating from the exhausts. In the last hour of darkness before dawn, the flotilla of five formed up, Number 4 leading; 1, the leader, last in the line as 'Tail-end Charlie'. The flotilla snaked silently ahead on electric motors, to leave the island on the starboard hand...

When the western tip of Pelampong was half a mile astern, Kyai turned. He pointed his bows into the channel and went slowly ahead to the northeast. The others formed up on him, on a line of bearing to port.

They stopped then, wallowing in the swell. It was very dark and Tim shivered: the last of the stars would soon be vanishing as twilight broke. Off to starboard, the steaming lights of a ship gleamed. As he watched, her lights opened, her bow light showing as she entered her turn round Raffles Light. She looked like a ULCC in ballast. She was huge, a black monster in the darkness.

CHAPTER TWENTY

Captain Johnny Hok, pilot, Port of Singapore Authority, had volunteered for this job; there had been no competition, for it entailed turning out at 0230 for the pilot boat. They had reached the Eastern Boarding Ground at 0415 and he had been hoisted up the power ladder on to the ULCC's deck at 0430. The Japanese ships were always punctual. Her master, Captain Yasuo Sato, was waiting for him on the bridge, shaven and immaculate in his tropical tunic. He bowed stiffly and welcomed the pilot to *Shoysa Maru*'s magnificent bridge. Johnny could understand the pride in the squat master's eyes: *Shoysa* was the second largest ULCC in the world, a miracle of modern engineering and electronics. She was permitted to pass through the Straits only when in ballast, returning loaded, via Lombok.

'You're drawing 13.6 metres, Captain, 14 aft?' Johnny said.

'So, pilot … plenty of water. It doesn't worry UKC.' They laughed politely: previous disasters had been caused by disregard of the statutory under-keel clearances. Memories were long.

'Happy to proceed, Captain? Twelve knots, if you please.'

Johnny Hok enjoyed his work, the friendliness, the old-world courtesies. There were few trades in which such traditions lingered. He checked her position on the chart, the soundings from the depth recorder. He watched the doppler log stealing up to twelve knots, then strolled across the length of her palatial bridge — more like the lounge of a modem hotel — and out to the starboard wing.

The light on St John was coming up abeam, flashing briefly its groups of two flashes, the ship was so close. Someone ahead was approaching in the other lane, but was well over on her side. It was exactly 0500 as St John slid past. The flood was still making satisfactorily, judging by the swirl against the pillar buoy.

The first sign of twilight was showing astern, a silver streak piercing the clouds of dawn rolling up from below the horizon. The forecast was good; there was a light breeze from the southwest, and visibility was tolerable for this time of the year. Johnny felt at ease, but not at peace: there had been no news of Cherry for ten days — and it was over a month since he'd heard from Tim... God, what a world. He'd never marry, that was for sure. Tim, poor devil, must be going through hell. Johnny dared not think of Cherry.

He watched with detachment a VLCC manoeuvring to the Esso terminal buoy off Gusong Tower. He returned into the subdued lighting of the wheelhouse. 'Eight knots, please, Captain, until we're past the VLCC.' He selected Channel 20 and passed the information through to Singapore Pilot. Gusong crept up abeam, half a mile to starboard. *Shoysa* slid past the seventeen-metre patch, and then Johnny knocked her up to twelve knots. He went to the chart and extracted his notebook to check his bearings: three miles only to 'wheel-over', for the 80°-turn round Raffles...

Johnny checked his port bow: three ships coming through the Phillip channel, their lights bright in the fading dawn. They were strung out, in a perfect line ahead, like a battle fleet of yore, on manoeuvres. The first two were entering the separation zone. The last must be just negotiating the worst bit, the four-cable channel off Takong Kechil. He leaned to swivel the azimuth ring and peered through the prism at the Raffles light, just fading in the dawn ... then a quick, double check on Takong...

'Stand by, sir...' Johnny walked briskly to the Decca and jotted down three readings for a rapid fix, then slashed the three crosscuts on the chart. They did not add up, complete nonsense... No time to take another. He returned to the azimuth ring. 'Wheel-over. Starboard twenty,' he ordered. He glanced at the sturdy captain peering through his binoculars. 'We're in the turn, captain. Cross bearings fit, but your Decca is defective.'

But all was well. Johnny had made this passage so often, with laden ships having minimal UKCs, that he could feel his way through this vital bottleneck. Extreme prudence was needed here, with a ship almost a quarter of a mile long — and he watched *Shoysa*'s massive bow sliding across the blur of the low lying land of the Malay Peninsula ... another 20° to swing for her course to take her safely out of the Main Channel ... 303°. He knew it by heart.

Ease to ten ... a rapid check on Raffles — 031° and 0530 exactly by the clock. About right, slightly ahead, just to port of the centre-line...

'Midships,' he called, intent now not to over-swing. 'Meet her.'

There was some activity going on around him, but he had learned long ago never to be distracted during the trickier moments. Captain Sato was strutting on his short legs to the far end of the windows; the officer of the watch was using his binoculars.

'Steady ... steer 303°.' Johnny supervised the quartermaster carefully: he never knew whether they understood the language. There was a fluttering sound above the bridge, making hearing difficult. The captain was shouting and pointing across the starboard bow.

'I'd like to push on now, captain,' the pilot said. Johnny had to average fifteen knots if she was to be at One Fathom Bank by dusk. He would have to reduce to twelve over Eastern Bank, but with fourteen metres draught, she could steam at sixteen in the main stretches — even at maximum squat. 'Captain…'

Sato was waving his hand, trying to attract attention. 'Boat, green two-o,' he snapped. 'She's flashing *Uniform*…' Johnny jerked the glasses to his eyes, picked up the launch in the murk of dawn. She was just visible, low freeboard. An Aldis lamp was flashing: 'U… U… U…'

Captain Sato shouted: 'Stop engines.' He strode to the radar. Johnny knocked back the throttle controls. Bloody maddening, just when he needed an accurate departure. This was obviously one of the newly formed UN patrols, officious as always, until they settled down. The winking red light of an aircraft showed in the low nimbus and then a large helicopter was swooping above the launch, flying towards *Shoysa*'s bows.

'Can't see anything,' Johnny reported, as he followed Sato to the starboard side of the wheelhouse. 'We're right for position, Captain, abeam of Pelampong and in the middle of the channel.' He had to repeat himself, but whether it was because Sato was excited or did not understand, he could not be sure. Outside, the fluttering sound had grown in intensity. It sounded like a chopper, but the big machine was still a hundred yards ahead and crossing the centreline. She had suddenly swooped to port and was coming in to hover above *Shoysa Maru*.

'What's going on, pilot?' Captain Sato asked, his jet eyes glaring at Johnny. 'I'm going outside.'

Johnny hurried after him. As he reached the starboard door, he saw Sato, his squat legs astride, peering and pointing upwards with astonishment, his other hand shielding his eyes from the first glare of the rising sun... The overwhelming cacophony of rotor blades fluttered directly overhead; a small helicopter, its bubble cockpit plainly visible, a rope dangling from its door, was swiftly climbing upwards. Johnny glimpsed the face of the pilot staring down at them unconcernedly. Sato was pointing angrily at another small chopper, which was already swooping across the starboard quarter of the poop deck. A rope was also dangling beneath its fuselage.

'Look out, sir...' someone shouted.

Johnny spun round. The officer of the watch was running towards the port door, holding his arms up in protest. There was a plume of smoke in the open rectangle of the door, the staccato rapping of an automatic weapon. A short figure stepped through, his face masked grotesquely, smoke curling from the barrel of his gun. The officer of the watch fell screaming, clutching at his stomach.

Things happened so rapidly that Johnny registered only the swift takeover of the entire bridge team. Sato had rushed in, running towards the radio-telephone. Another burst cut him down, but this time it originated from the starboard door behind Johnny. He was aware that two men were in the wheelhouse, one at the central console, the other covering the three engineers who were now standing against the back of the bridge. The terrorists spoke in Japanese at the terrified helmsman and swung their guns on Johnny. The helmsman stepped aside, pointing to the wheel. The larger of the two grabbed Johnny, shoved him on the steering. The man pointed for'd, jerking his thumb, pointing to the westward to where the black conical buoy guarding Kent rocks should have been. He twiddled his free hand, pointing to the engine throttles. Johnny jumped towards them and pushed the revs up to twelve knots…

As Johnny took the wheel again, he saw that a large helicopter was landing on the chopper spot, two-thirds up the length of the deck, on the port side. Dark bundles were tumbling out through its door. Four men in dark green uniform were scrambling along the deck and lugging their loads to the ship's rail. They attached hooks to the top rail, slashed at the ties; and then the jumping ladders uncoiled and fell over the port side. A fifth man, in the corner by the breakwater, was covering operations with his automatic.

The two terrorists on the bridge were exchanging sharp sentences with each other, their eyes darting towards the for'd windows. A telephone buzzed on the engine-room panel, the red light blinking. The tall guard nodded at the engineer on watch. The white-faced man in white overalls stepped forward and snatched at the instrument. He looked over his shoulder at Johnny, hesitated, then shouted in pidgin Japanese.

'There's a hijacker in the engine room — we can see him on the television monitor … and the lift's guarded. No one can leave the accommodation island.'

'Okay,' Johnny snapped. 'See what you can do about your captain. Ask them in Japanese whether they'll allow you to help him.'

He watched the engineer talking to the guard and saw the man nod. Sato was moaning where he lay, but he was conscious and staring dazedly at the drama about him. Johnny checked the doppler log — twelve knots — and he was on course again. Still no sign of the buoy, but he could just pick out Sultan Shoal lighthouse on the starboard bow. He glimpsed through the port doorway and saw the surf of Palempong and Kent rocks passing down the port quarter.

'Tell them to put the helmsman back on the wheel,' he shouted at the engineer. 'How the hell can I navigate?' He glanced at the clock: 0549. With his free hand he wrenched his navigator's notebook from his shirt pocket and flicked it open. Eleven minutes, then, to 'wheel-over' for the next course into the entrance to the Malacca Strait — 284°. Sultan Shoal was coming up broad now — and then he saw a swarm of men running down the upper deck, far below.

Eight ladders were hooked to the rail, in groups of four, and the last of the hijackers were vaulting across to rig some sort of mechanical hoist between the two forward pairs of ladders. The men in jungle green were disappearing beneath the accommodation island. The deck was swarming with them. They seemed to know their business, single individuals breaking away to take up vantage points along the deck.

The fo'c'sle lookout was in for a shock … and then Johnny realized that the launch, the bastard who had flashed the 'U', had vanished. Not surprising — only twenty-two minutes had elapsed since the start of this wretched business — then he felt the Japanese quartermaster taking over the steering again. Johnny dashed to the chart table and began trying another Decca fix.

He had taken the first reading, but could not get a second — nor a third. The bloody thing was on the blink. He rushed to the radar, stuck his head inside the visor. At least this was still working, the strobe rotating serenely, painting its echoes: a ship seven miles to the nor-westward, Ajax Shoal showing clearly with its distinctive racon, the identifiable radar beacon. Another four minutes before altering…

Johnny jerked from the visor as he heard the door slamming against the bulkhead. He spun round to face a posse of soldiers, all in the same dark green uniforms. A heap of them, enough to take over the *Ark Royal*, exploded into the wheelhouse, fanned out, took up their positions. As Johnny watched, their leader, a tall, ugly-looking brute, strode into the wheelhouse, an automatic pistol in his hand. He marched straight towards Johnny.

'We've taken over this ship,' he barked, in perfect English, 'in the name of the People's Liberation Army of East Asia. My name is Tumelaka, commander of the Red Dragons Western Division.' He threw a bundled flag to a soldier at the door. As it unrolled, Johnny saw the outline of a red dragon, fire issuing from its nostrils, emblazoned upon a green ground. 'You're the pilot?'

'I am. You've mortally wounded the captain.'

Tumelaka strode to the captain's body, which was now propped against the port side of the wheelhouse. His eyes were open, but a dark stain welled from beneath his body where he sat. The terrorist leader bent over and spat in his face. Then he turned to Johnny. 'Can you navigate this ship on your own?'

The pilot shrugged his shoulders. 'Navigate her, yes. But run her — she needs her ship's officers.' He pointed to the twisted corpse lying close to the radar pedestal. 'You won't get far without her officers.'

'I haven't far to go.' Tumelaka's laughter was high-pitched, with a note of hysteria. Johnny's hair bristled at the nape of his neck. Tumelaka turned to the group at the back of the wheelhouse, singled out one of the sergeants, said something to him and drew his fingers across his own throat. The sergeant marched out, beckoning his section to follow.

'I'm sparing the chief engineer,' Tumelaka said. 'We can do without the rest, except for the chief officer. I'll need him too.' He turned to Johnny: 'Where are we?'

'I've got to alter course,' Johnny said, taking a bearing of Sultan light. '*Now…*' He was two minutes late already: 0602. He spoke directly to the helmsman. 'Port ten, steer 284° … 284°, understand?'

The helmsman nodded; another hour on this course, and she'd be up to Pulau Iju-ketjil, where *Shoysa Maru* would steady on the long haul for One Fathom Bank.

'Give me your radio-telephone,' the terrorist leader shouted.

Johnny strolled to the instrument placed in the centre of the bridge control. 'What channel? Whom d'you want to speak to?'

'Your top people…'

'Singapore Radio, then. We're still within range. Channel 16 — You'll reach the world, all right. It's everyone's frequency.' Johnny held the phone for the terrorist. 'Press the button when you want to speak…'

Tumelaka beckoned to another of his sergeants. 'Bring the Englishman here.'

There was a scuffle at the back of the bridge. Another sergeant, a tall, lean Malay man, yanked at a short cord, jerking a prisoner to the centre of the bridge. The wretched fellow stumbled, head down, barely able to walk. Then he halted abruptly in front of his tormentor. He slowly braced his broad shoulders, his bound wrists resisting the tugging of the cord.

Looking Tumelaka straight in the face, he spoke without raising his voice: 'You bloody murderer.' He was rigid, waiting for the bullet, the crashing blow. And in that second, behind the red beard, Johnny Hok recognized his sister's boyfriend. The short, stubby man had guts… His dignity in this frightening pantomime reassured Johnny in the silence that followed.

Tumelaka was fingering his holster, twitching from one foot to the other. He grabbed Simkins by the collar of his shirt. He shouted to the Malay sergeant: 'Tell the boats to shove off...' He snatched the phone from Johnny: 'Give me Channel 16.' He dragged his prisoner to the telephone. 'When I say so,' he snapped, 'tell them you've seen your girlfriend. Tell 'em Miss Hok's alive and well.' He released Simkins, slipped the gun from his holster and cocked it.

'Singapore Radio, Singapore Radio, Singapore Radio, this is ULCC *Shoysa Maru*...' Johnny was calling into the R/T.

The unreality of the nightmare robbed Johnny's mind of rational thought. He caught Tim's eye, registered the mutual recognition, and surreptitiously twitched a smile.

He peered through the window at the tanker's immense bow ploughing serenely through the calm sea. Off the port bow, a flotilla of four fast attack craft, all heavily gunned, were belting off to the westward. Their wakes boiled, threshing white; across the transom of the last launch, he could distinguish the number 1 painted in black.

CHAPTER TWENTY-ONE

They were already sitting down at the table when Yong hastened into the Prime Minister's personal office at seven-fifteen on that Thursday morning. He had been woken by the phone an hour earlier. A worried Port of Singapore Authority watchkeeper had garbled something about an emergency in the Strait concerning an ULCC. He had refused to say more, only that Yong had better get round to the PM's office immediately.

'Take a chair, Yong...'

His boss, the Minister for Home Affairs, looked worried, as he chatted quietly with the Minister for Defence, the police chief listening attentively. A secretary was setting up a tape recorder on the Prime Minister's desk. Yong sat down at the end of the table. The PM was evidently taking the chair himself. Yong breathed a sigh of relief: the meeting would be brief.

'Sit down, gentlemen,' the Prime Minister said quietly. 'We've not moment to lose, I understand...' He cocked an eye at his Defence Minister. Yong watched them taking their places: the Minister for Defence on the Prime Minister's right, Home Affairs on the left. Around the rest of the circular table were distributed the defence chiefs and the UN chief of the Strait Patrol Force. Even the police chief, normally case-hardened by the worst monstrosities, seemed anxious.

'Listen to this recording,' Home Affairs said. 'PSA received it at 0607. It speaks for itself, gentlemen.' He nodded to the secretary. The cassette hummed, then cut in. Above the background of routine procedure in the PSA signal station, a high-pitched male voice began talking in an Indonesian accent.

'…Singapore Radio… This is ULCC *Shoysa Maru, Shoysa Maru, Shoysa Maru.*'

'*Shoysa Maru* … good morning. This is Singapore Radio. Pass your message, please.'

There was an unintelligible scuffling in the background, then the voice cut in again. 'I have an urgent message to be recorded. Tell me when you're ready.'

'We're ready, your message is being recorded. Speak now…'

'I am broadcasting from the bridge of the Japanese ULCC, *Shoysa Maru,* In the name of the People's Liberation Army of East Asia, the ship is now the property of the Red Dragons. I, Tumelaka, have taken control of the ship which is now proceeding northwest through the Malacca Strait. Her position is, according to the Singapore pilot, in the centre of the channel south of Sultan Shoal lighthouse… Her course is 284, speed sixteen. D'you read me, Singapore?'

Another crackle and then the startled voice of the morning watchkeeper in the signal tower cut in: 'Go ahead, *Shoysa Maru,* Message received.'

The hijacker's voice again: 'High Command have authorized me to read its ultimatum to you: "The Liberation Army has lost patience with the renewed negotiations over the Hok ransom. The Red Dragon Army no longer believes in the good faith of the capitalist negotiators. In consequence, the following demands must be met by 1800 today, repeat, 1800 *today*.

"'One: Immediate release of Liberation Army fighters illegally imprisoned — nine in Japan; seven in Italy; eight in Western Germany; two in Singapore. Those under sentence of death in Changi, Singapore, to be guaranteed safe conduct to the Malay frontier."'

Yong glanced at the faces before him, all clamped, like vices. The melodramatic voice from the cassette was continuing.

"'Two: Ten million US dollars in gold to be lowered by helicopter to the deck of *Shoysa Maru*.'"

Someone whistled softly at the end of the table.

"'Three: the following agreements to be made legally binding in the International Court. A: Japan to stop her naval programme. Her fleet to remain at its present size. B: Papua New Guinea to be liberated and political power returned to its people by the Government of Australia. C: The Malacca and Singapore Straits to be declared in Indonesia's, Malaysia's and Singapore's Exclusive Economic Zone. The Straits are therefore in territorial waters and are not High Seas.'"

The spokesman paused and there was a low humming over the air. Then he came in again.

'Are you recording? Do you hear me, Singapore?' For the first time, he sounded unsure of himself. He coughed and went on: 'Your governments have until 1800 tonight, I repeat, until 1800, to agree to and to meet the conditions of our ultimatum. If you refuse, *Shoysa Maru* will be sunk in the Strait.' He repeated slowly: 'You have until six o'clock tonight.

'If any attempt is made to re-capture the ship, two actions will immediately result — Miss Hok will be executed. The ship will be sunk. The scuttling charges are being placed at this moment...' There was another pause, someone was muttering alongside.

'Communications will be on International Frequency 2182, which will be guarded continually. Red Dragon High Command is also in contact with you on this frequency from South Vietnam. They await your acknowledgement. Singapore ... Singapore, have you received my message?'

'This is Singapore Radio. Message received, *Shoysa Maru*...'

'Stand by, Singapore. I have a further message for you...' Once again, that scuffling and then the sound of breathing as someone broke in: 'Singapore Radio... This is Captain Timothy Simkins ... Simkins, ex-chief officer *Baitulla*. I was running London Shipping Singapore office.' There was a grunt, an intake of breath, then the voice went on.

'I am speaking to you ... to emphasize that these terrorists are in deadly earnest. *Shoysa Maru* has been hijacked. I have seen Miss Hok ... and ... she's ... she's alive, in the hands of the Red Dragons. This is not a hoax ... OUT.'

The cassette clicked, then slurred into silence.

The Prime Minister was the first to speak. He turned to David Sen, his private secretary, a man in his thirties. 'Get the American and Russian ambassadors here at once. Tell them I expect them here in ten minutes, shaved or not.'

David Sen rushed from the room as the Prime Minister opened the discussion. Yong helped when he could, giving details of his most recent negotiations with the kidnappers: he had been worried in the early hours by reports coming in of possible terrorist activities at sea, for fast craft had been picked up on the Malay Peninsula's coastal radar. There were inexplicable failures of the navigational aids along the coast. No one had been able to contact One Fathom Bank lighthouse yet...

'We heard of the collision in the southeast lane only a few hours ago,' the navy chief said. 'Kelang's lifeboat's searching for survivors.'

'Why haven't I been told about this?' the PM asked, glaring at his Defence Minister. 'Brief details...?'

Yong felt sympathy for the defence people — the accident had happened only about five hours ago and communications were erratic.

'The RO/RO has sunk close to the 1972 wreck, sir. A sheep-ship has run up on the bank, but I think her stern is in the fairway.'

'Does that mean the southeast lane at One Fathom Bank is blocked to deep draught ships?' The PM's voice was deceptively calm.

The navy chief drummed the table with his fingertips. 'Yes, sir… We've got to close it.'

Yong watched the second hand of the clock above the Prime Minister's head. Remorselessly it crept around the dial, a full twenty seconds, before anyone spoke.

'A terrible thing to happen — just at this moment…' The Prime Minister struck the table. 'You know what this means, gentlemen?'

The navy chief replied lamely for them all: 'The hijackers may not know that the lane's blocked, sir.'

The Home Affairs Minister glanced briefly at his police chief, then spoke to the sailor: 'They'll know by now, John. You can bank on it.'

'I've dispatched our emergency patrol boat,' the admiral said. 'The flotilla will be leaving harbour within the hour. The UN patrol's coming down from Kelang.'

'Their orders?'

'To shadow and report. On no account attempt to board.'

'I should hope not,' the PM snapped. 'What are you doing, Air Marshal?'

'Scrambling the Hunters, sir. The Skyhawks are bombing up.'

'The choppers?'

'Two waves of Alouettes, sir. First squadron is readying now.'

The Prime Minister jumped to his feet and strode to the chart which covered the whole of one wall.

'What the hell can we do, Chua?' He turned in exasperation to his Defence Chief. 'They've got us.'

'Quite so…'

The meeting gathered round the chart, the best brains in Singapore, Yong knew. The admiral was running his finger along the route between the northern tip of Long Bank and Pyramid Shoal. 'Seventy-five miles, sir, of deeper water. Then another thirty-five, till One Fathom Bank.'

'There's a wreck off South Sands,' the PM reminded them. 'That tanker which polluted Port Dickson — remember, in the spring?'

'The first stretch of deep water is the best, then, sir…'

No one voiced their thoughts. Then the Prime Minister spoke. 'Okay, so we sink her here —' and he stabbed his finger north of Long Bank. 'The Strait won't be closed, but we will have deliberately sunk a foreign ship and that's an act of war.'

'Our Japanese friends would be the first to agree with you, sir.'

'— and we'd be responsible for the butchering of *Shoysa*'s crew?'

'And the killing of Miss Hok, sir,' Yong added quietly.

The door opened, held by the breathless private secretary.

The Prime Minister led the ambassadors straight to the chart. 'Mr Sen has already given you the outline of what's going on,' he said. 'We've been discussing it here. Without your help, gentlemen, there's nothing we can do. We can't capture her or they'll sink her; they'll butcher the crew and their hostage. Get through to your masters,' he stormed. 'Do everything you can — and fast.' He took them by the arm and began shoving them towards the door.

'If these hijackers close the Strait at One Fathom Bank,' the American told his opposite number, 'there'll be anarchy in

Japan and most of these parts. Misery and anarchy, your prescription for the world.' He laughed bitterly.

The Russian turned, his grey face flushing. 'Mr Ambassador,' he snapped. 'The Soviet Navy depends on the free passage of these Straits just as much as the Americans. I will contact Moscow immediately.' He pushed his way through the door.

The Prime Minister shrugged his shoulders and smiled bleakly at the American ambassador. 'Tell your President to use the hotline,' he said. He glanced at his watch. 'It's almost eight o'clock.'

'We've got the *Ike* off Hainan,' the American said briskly. 'We'll get off a strike of Phantoms, if you will allow them to land here, sir.'

'Thanks, Wayne. Do that.'

The PM turned and slowly closed the door on the departing diplomats.

'For once they share a common interest,' the Defence Minister said shortly.

'But what can they do?' The Prime Minister shrugged in resignation. 'When will they ever learn? Force, even in this situation, can do nothing, absolutely nothing. Get through to the ULCC. Let's see if she's still afloat.'

CHAPTER TWENTY-TWO

Captain Hok was leaning upon the forward ledge of the wheelhouse and gazing along the length of the deck running almost to the horizon line. Since the telephone conversation at 0845, things had grown more tense, particularly after clearing the tip of Long Bank.

The terrorist leader was slumped morosely in the captain's chair. His silence was reflected throughout the bridge, where small groups of his troops smoked. They were taking time to reflect, particularly after the R/T announcement by the Minister of Home Affairs at 0845: without committing his allies, the Government of the Republic of Singapore repudiated absolutely the hijackers' ultimatum. Piracy, even when carried out in territorial waters, would be punished by the laws of that country in which piracy was committed. When *Shoysa Maru* cleared the Malacca Strait, she would be arrested on the High Seas by the first warship available … *of whatever nationality* — and then the Minister's calm voice had added that the Soviets and the Americans had been requested to help. Meanwhile, the ULCC would be shadowed during her passage up the Strait.

Tumelaka excitedly acknowledged the message and, shortly afterwards, a message from the Red Dragon headquarters came up on the same frequency. 'Take the consequences,' he had snapped. 'You still have nine hours.' He shut down again.

Johnny Hok tried to ignore the pandemonium around him. Johnny, as pilot of this ULCC, had no navigational aids to help him. The radio beacons were being jammed, so D/F was denied him; and the radar reflectors on the buoys seemed to be missing, some of the buoys having disappeared altogether. Decca was giving no signal at all, so he was forced to run a DR on radar bearings.

The doppler log was working and, he hoped, was accurate, as he was accepting her speed as sixteen knots during the deeper stretches, averaging fifteen for the passage to One Fathom Bank. He had breathed a sigh of relief after altering safely to 300° when Pulau Iju-ketjil was due south at 0705; *Shoysa Maru* could not have cleared the wreck in the middle of the channel off Kukup island by much... Then at 0800 he had settled on 302° for the run through to the approaches to the northwest lane at One Fathom Bank.

Malacca Radio came through with a report that the southeast lane was closed by an early morning collision; all traffic would be using the northwest lane; extreme caution must be exercised. Hok was not amused: the width in the narrowest section for the deep draught stuff was less than ten cables — and *Shoysa*'s beam was almost half a cable. Another VLCC being forced to come south through the same lane with the tide under her would certainly give *Shoysa* a problem.

Hok glanced again at the log: if he could maintain sixteen knots, he would have got his 'tidal window' right and arrive at One Fathom Bank on the last of the flood or, at worst, slack water. He was also broadcasting hourly his position to the Director of Marine, Singapore; he had finally managed to persuade Tumelaka that this routine was essential for the safe navigation of the ship.

The 0940 broadcast had driven Tumelaka berserk. The Americans had scrambled a squadron of Phantoms from their carrier, *Eisenhower*, somewhere to the eastward. The hot line was being used between Washington and Moscow: the Kremlin, for once, was in full accord and was using its influence where it counted. Tumelaka's frenzy worried Johnny: in a panic, Tumelaka had rushed round the upper deck himself to ensure that his troops were fully alert, disposed in the best tactical positions.

Tumelaka had returned to the bridge, his eyes blazing: 'Traitors, traitors,' he was mouthing to himself. And it was then, steaming serenely through the calm sea under a cloudless, sultry sky, that he had mustered all *Shoysa*'s crew on the upper deck, ahead of the breakwater, but abaft the helicopter spot on the port side. Standing on the scorching steel beneath the burning sun, they were roped to the centre-line catwalk. The two machine-gunners, installed strategically in the angle by the main manifolds, covered them with their weapons, at the same time marking the bridge. Then all the officers, except the chief engineer and the mate, were lined up outside the starboard wheelhouse door. Two men stood in front of them, legs astride, their automatic weapons aimed at the officers' stomachs.

'Switch on the radio-telephone,' Tumelaka shouted.

'It's on, it has been all the time,' Hok said.

The terrorist grabbed the phone and pressed the transmit switch. Johnny could look no more. He tried to divorce himself from this nightmare and concentrate on his navigating. He focused on the operator's cabin at the top of the starboard crane pedestal. A terrorist officer had been manning this position ever since the scuttling charges were laid immediately after the capture. Taking the mate with them, they unreeled the electric cable from a spool carried by two soldiers. They descended into the seven selected cargo tanks, starting right forward.

Johnny could see the black cable running along the deck and branching off into the seven deck hatches. The after branch connection continued out of sight beneath the bridge — probably running to the engine room. The circuit terminated in the crane cabin, where presumably the terrorist kept his hand on the detonator firing plunger... Johnny had been horrified by the size of the charges they had lowered down into the empty tanks; their diameters only just slipped through the hatchways.

'*Pilot...*' Tumelaka was shouting at him. 'Are you sure this is working?'

'It's live... You're on the air.'

Tumelaka began talking rapidly into the phone; if the scene had not been so tragic, it would have been difficult to keep a straight face. 'Singapore, do you read?'

'Come in, *Shoysa.*'

'You people don't think we're serious...' He laughed loudly. 'Listen to this...' He turned to the sentries on the starboard wing. 'Fire! Kill them!' he shouted.

The guns stuttered, the screams shattering the soughing of the breeze outside.

'D'you understand now, Singapore? We're serious. Tell that to your masters... Out.' He thrust the phone into Hok's hand. 'Where are we now?'

'Formosa Bank. We're in deeper water.'

'Message received,' a calm voice came through on the loudspeaker.

Lieutenant Tan Sri Rajaratnam, Republic of Singapore Navy, had been sitting in the cockpit of Alouette number 112, of 24 Helicopter Squadron, for over half an hour. All the pre-takeoff checks had been completed and the crew were bored with waiting. The three heavy steel boxes had been stored at the back, by the rear door; the lowering cable had been checked, and the thirty fathoms of rope, attached to each box and to a marker buoy, had been carefully coiled. The sun was cooking him through the plastic cockpit and their flying suits and helmets didn't help … and then control came in: 'Take off.'

The engine whined and the rotor 'choffed' invisibly. 'Lifting … torque coming in.'

He pulled in the collective lever and applied power as he counteracted the increased torque by gently pushing his foot on the yaw pedals. He played with the cyclic to take her up vertically.

'Torque is good,' Lim, his co-pilot, monitored, 'seventy-five percent. NR 102. Temperatures and pressures all good. Captions clear, landing gear coming up. Compass aligned…'

Tan pulled her up and away to the westward.

'Clear to the left,' the co-pilot sang out.

Tan applied power and took the helicopter up to 3,000 feet, the city and the island slipping away beneath them. His orders were simple: find the hijacked ULCC which was on her way up to One Fathom Bank, shadow her and, when ordered, hover, then land the boxes on her spot which was sited on her port side. He noted the time on his kneepad as the chopper crossed the coast, the turquoise sea breaking lazily along the shores: 1147. The ULCC's position was reported as approaching Rob Roy Bank, so he ought to make contact within the hour.

'Opening heading 254°,' Lim said. 'That'll clear Piai Point.'

'Roger … 254°.'

Tan pushed her nose forward and lifted her up, testing for the first time the maximum power. He monitored the torque gauge, while Lim checked the gas generator speed and the turbine inlet temperatures.

'Power good,' he said. 'Torque limiting, 110…'

And so the flight continued. Tan felt the bump when the baralt came in, and then he settled down for the chase. This was beating the book, after the monotony of the last month.

It was 1228 when Lim saw the first herring-bones of *Shoysa's* wash, a mini ship, 3,000 feet below. She was encircled by a flotilla of small ships, each of their wakes mottled streaks in the glistening sea. 'Keep clear until you're ordered in,' the CO had emphasized. 'Shadow until we're sure. Any nonsense and they'll knock you out of the sky.'

So Tan took her down to forty feet above the sea, keeping to the southward of the tanker standing up like a gargantuan barge with her orange paint. He had to make twenty knots to maintain bearing; when he was settled, he called up base: 'Shadowing. In position, seven miles south of ship. My speed of advance sixteen knots.'

Tan felt the excitement heightening as he piloted his Alouette carefully up the Strait, well within Indonesian waters. Lim had his eyes skinned, for he never knew with these people. *Shoysa Maru* was ploughing along, looking for all the world like a normal ship. The only unusual thing was the armada escorting her, an assortment of patrol craft maintaining station on her at about five miles on either side. And, far over to the westward, a line of FACs tucked in against the land, out of sight from the big ship and her shadowers. Then he saw the gleam in the sunlight, the flicker of light upon the wings of the fighters flashing past: those must be the Phantoms, and even from here he could see the white star in the blue circle, with the two horizontal lines... The US Navy had turned up.

Base was talking. The matter-of-fact voice of the controller said, 'Proceed in execution of previous orders. Good luck.'

'Here we go, Lim. Stand by at the back. We're going in.'

They skimmed at forty feet across the surface, closed on a 120° track. Tan judged it perfectly, bringing her up nicely, off her port bow. He went into the hover, checked by instrument that the chopper was into the wind.

He edged towards the huge slab side, glimpsed the mountain of water, a black whorl surging ahead of the bulb. Then he saw the soldiers. A machine gun was trained on the chopper and men were aiming their automatic weapons.

'Friendly reception,' Tan muttered. 'Okay — here we go. Open the door; stand by to lower.'

All his senses alert, he concentrated entirely on the flying. This was easy, compared to landing on some ships: this monster had no break in the foredeck — only the back eddies over the bows. He twitched her ahead, a touch more nose down — up with the torque … and then he was hovering, keeping spot-on for relative position.

'Thirty feet,' Lim monitored. 'Temperatures and pressures good.'

'Lower the boxes.'

'Right.'

He waited for each report, each box on deck, unattached. Soldiers were running beneath, disappearing beneath the cab…

'All boxes clear.'

A kick of relief, and Tan began lifting her, putting the ball 2° lower… There was a yell from Lim. Tan glanced downwards, saw the length of rope spiralling towards the deck, the orange buoy tumbling after it.

'Shit,' Lim shouted through his intercom. 'We've dropped one of the marker buoys.'

Tan spotted the tracer streaming from the machine gun tucked in by the winches. It seemed to arc slowly towards them. As the chopper canted across the ship's rail, he felt a thud from back aft. There was a shattering *bang!* And then his world spiralled into chaos.

'The tail's gone,' Tan yelled. The helicopter suddenly began whirling round upon itself, out of control. Their world spun wildly, entirely disorientating them. In seconds, she was falling from the sky, half on her side. He cut the engine.

'*Brace … brace … brace…*'

As they hit, he saw a black wave, a huge thing from the tanker's bow, rearing to overwhelm them. The machine hung for a second, the whirling rotor tips touched the sea and then they were spinning upside down. A sudden gloom overwhelmed them and they were fighting for their lives.

Tan slipped his safety belt, took a deep breath, and banged the emergency window with his elbow... He kicked desperately... There was a suffocating pain in his chest, a roaring in his ears, then the black night … and he knew no more.

CHAPTER TWENTY-THREE

It was exactly two hours after the hijackers shot down the helicopter that Tokyo capitulated to the Red Dragon's ultimatum. Tim, from his cramped wretchedness at the back of the engine room control area, listened to the loudspeaker, being relayed through Port Dickson now, announcing the news. Perhaps the authorities now admitted the reality of the situation? Tumelaka had executed one member of the crew at each hour, as he had threatened he would, until some concession was made. They had stopped bothering to bring the condemned man up to the bridge, and every hour Tim heard the shot from for'd. He was counting the hours by each execution. Tim realized that Tumelaka was taking his orders from Red Dragon High Command, for frequently the same sharp, Japanese accent would come on the air, breaking into the radio traffic. And the latest atrocity, the hourly shooting, had been ordered from ashore. It must be three o'clock, for there had been another shot.

Tim's head was swimming, the bridge reeling about him where he sat, his back against the port bulkhead. He was fighting despair, yet it would have been a release if Tumelaka had put a bullet through him. He had not eaten for hours, though the hijackers had disappeared in shifts to the mess hall below, where the ship's chefs were forced to provide food. The terrorists certainly had the operation organized, even to the extent of delivering trays of the stuff to the guards around the ship.

Tim dared not think about Cherry. The last time he had allowed his mind to wander to her, he had lost control and tried to get at the bastard as he'd strutted close past him. Hamzah had restrained him, jumping in front of him to shield the madness. Hamzah was never far off; at that moment he was slouched in the opposite corner, apparently dozing. Tumelaka was settled in the captain's chair. The wretched Japanese captain had died, and they had dumped his body over the side.

Suddenly, Tim felt a wave of nausea sweep over him. He struggled, trying to catch Hamzah's eye. Then the pilot, grey with tiredness, saw his plight. Johnny went over to Tumelaka and pointed at Tim. The pirate barked at the bunch of lounging guards. Hamzah jerked to his feet and went over to Tim.

Tim felt his bindings loosened and then he was hauled from the wheelhouse. Hamzah pushed open the heads door at the rear of the bridge complex, and stayed with Tim while he was violently sick. Then Hamzah went to the door and wedged his gun under the handle. As he helped Tim clean up, he spoke rapidly: 'Tumelaka will sink her. He's mad. He'll grab Miss Hok for himself. He longs for revolution. He'll cause as much havoc as he can. I'm certain he means to sink this ship. He's got his fast attack craft standing by. They'll run in at the last moment to take off himself and the troops.'

'But will he ignore orders from shore?' Tim whispered. 'They've got the ten million dollars already. Japan has given in. There's still time for the other nations.'

'Tumelaka's a fanatic. He'll disregard orders — or he'll find some pretext. I'm certain of that.'

'What are we going to do?'

'If all goes Tumelaka's way,' Jaafar said, 'I'll shoot him as he goes over the side. Mine was the first wave in — it's the last one out. I quit with Tumelaka, covering him.' He smiled at

Tim. 'Feeling better?' He went to the door, kicked away the gun, and stayed with his back against the door. 'I don't care if I die now, Tim. But I'll get Tumelaka first.'

'I'm with you,' Tim said, feeling his strength returning. 'But get me some food. Cut my bindings when you need me.'

'I'll slip you a gun. I'll give you time.'

'Jaafar…' Tim's mind was working again, with the hope of action at last. 'How valuable is that bastard to the Red Dragons?'

'The Sumatran front would collapse without him.'

'As valuable as that? Why don't we trade him, if we can grab him at the last moment? We could barter him for Cherry.'

Hamzah sucked the air softly through his teeth. 'I'm the last to be with him, his rearguard. But we'll lose the ship. Each charge is time-fused. They'll be set for the last moment, when Tumelaka shuts the survivors in the engine room.'

'We've got to warn Hok. Here, quick, give me a pen.'

Tim scrawled a couple of sentences on a paper towel. Jaafar stuffed it into his pocket. 'Okay, I'll get it to him,' he whispered. 'Better get going…' He lashed Tim's hands again. 'There're still another few hours to go… I'll get you something to eat. Collect your strength.'

They could hear the rumpus from the wheelhouse. Hamzah wrenched at the door and shoved Tim into the passage. As they entered the bridge, Tim was pushed savagely from behind. He crashed into the shadowy corner, the engineer officer's desk between him and the bridge control.

He listened to Hok arguing sarcastically with Tumelaka. The pilot was insisting on reducing to twelve knots while the ship negotiated the patches off Cape Rachado.

'I'll knock her up again after Pyramid shoal at 1600. There's a fresh wreck we must leave on our port hand. Ever heard of "squat", Tumelaka?' Tim wondered how Hok was getting away with it.

'Port Dickson Radio, this is Port Dickson Radio…'

'Pass your message…' Hok said.

'Important message for hijackers. Message begins —' the operator nervously cleared his throat — 'From Singapore Command, message begins — American and Russian governments state they will use every influence at their command to obtain pardon for terrorist prisoners held in countries designated. This solemn guarantee will be honoured once *Shoysa Maru* is clear of One Fathom Bank and is west, repeat west of meridian 100, repeat meridian 100.' Tim could hear only the crackling of the loudspeaker. 'Please acknowledge,' the voice concluded. 'Message ends.' There was a click — then only the background noise.

Tumelaka leaped out of his seat. As he grabbed the radiotelephone, the air shook; there was a bang and a deafening roar… Shadows flickered past the starboard doorway and then the Phantoms were gone, twisting and turning, their exhausts leaving plumes of smoke in the sky.

CHAPTER TWENTY-FOUR

Port Dickson Radio passed the message at 1658: the Australian Government flatly refused to negotiate with the terrorists. And as Johnny Hok replaced the radiotelephone, he turned wearily to watch the reaction of the scoundrel sitting silent and motionless in the captain's chair. Tumelaka remained rigid, his face twitching, his fingers clenching the upholstered arms spasmodically. He was staring straight through the window along the length of the deck — and that was when Hok finally knew that the game was over: nothing could prevent the impending catastrophe now.

Johnny Hok had been conning *Shoysa Mara* for over twelve hours. The diminutive helmsman was out on his feet, but between them they had succeeded in scraping past the wreck of *Sula*, that tanker breaking up on the bank north of Pyramid Shoal. The bridge clock was just tinging its 'two bells': five o'clock at last — and, he supposed, time for another execution. The evening was already closing in, the sun an orange ball behind the bank of cumuli rising over the mountain ranges of Northern Sumatra a hundred miles to the west.

There had been very little shipping coming down from the northwest: presumably, the authorities had warned east-going masters to stay north of One Fathom Bank until the crisis was over. The navigational warnings had been pushed out every half hour, a flood which Johnny ignored. What mattered was the next two hours: One Fathom Bank lighthouse was completely out of action, its lights, its racon (always unreliable) and its communications were not functioning. The new light beacons were extinguished and the buoys at the northern entrance to the channel were reported missing. A light with identical characteristics (flashing every five seconds) had been reported off the dumping ground, and should be treated with caution…

Hok dragged himself across to the radar once again. The D/F stations were being jammed out and Decca was US, so *Shoysa*'s safe transit now depended solely on the reliability of the radar. He watched the points and identified them for the umpteenth time upon the shore marks: Jemur and the Aruahs were where they should be; the island of Senebui showing abeam to port; the hill of Jugra to starboard on the Malay Peninsula foreshore; the entrance to Kelang, 050° — and, most important of all, the lighthouse structures of One Fathom Bank; its two satellites, one partially built, the other in ruins, were close to the main light which bore 310°. He was on the line, but perhaps ten minutes behind his DR. He would make no adjustment, for *Shoysa* was about right for the tail of the central separation zone. As he was marking '1717' on the chart against the fix, the loudspeaker cut in.

'This is Red Dragon High Command…'

Tumelaka jumped to his feet and paced across to the telephone. 'This is *Shoysa Maru*… Pass your message.'

'Execute Phase Two… Execute Phase Two.' The clipped voice, the same one which had been directing operations all day, was devoid of emotion. 'Acknowledge…'

'This is *Shoysa*,' Tumelaka grinned. 'Execute Phase Two acknowledged, repeat, acknowledged — out.' He slammed the phone back in its rest. He strode back to the centre of the bridge and snapped the switch on the ship's intercom. 'Your commander speaking: take all the ship's crew to the lower engine-room compartment. Lock them below, as previously exercised.'

'Okay, Commander.' Hok recognized the second-in-command's voice, the butcher who had directed most of the killings. The miserable survivors were goaded aft until they disappeared behind the accommodation island. Hok flung off Tumelaka's grasp.

'What d'you want with me?'

'Come to the chart. If you bungle this, I'll put a bullet through you myself.'

Hok was beyond all feeling as he crouched over the chart table. Tumelaka extracted a tracing of the separation zone from his pocket and smoothed it upon the section covering One Fathom Bank. A cross circled in red was marked just south of Amazon Maru shoal.

'There,' Tumelaka said, stubbing the point with his finger. 'Anchor the ship in exactly this position.'

Hok laid off the anchorage: 177° One Fathom Bank lighthouse 3.2 miles. 'I'll need time to work out my anchor bearings.' He glanced up at the man standing over him. 'We'll be off the entrance to the separation zone at 1800. I'll have to turn to stem the tide.'

'Drop the anchor *there*. That's all you have to do.' Tumelaka's face was glistening with exultation; beads of sweat shone at his temples as he straightened his beret. He went back to the intercom and spoke in Indonesian to his Number One.

'Who's to anchor the ship?' Hok shouted angrily. 'There aren't any seamen left.'

Tumelaka was grinning as he turned. 'The Englishman,' he barked. 'I've kept him for this. He's a sailor, isn't he?'

Johnny Hok stole a glance at the exhausted man slumped asleep in the corner. The Malay guard, who was pacing silently to and fro across the back of the bridge, met his eye and nodded imperceptibly. Hok continued with his anchor plan, laying off his bearings: everything depended upon whether he could identify his objects. He must, he knew, catch the last of the twilight and the tide. Twilight ended at 1831, so he must maintain sixteen knots as long as he could.

When he finished, it was already 1730. In half an hour, if he was on time for his DR, he would make a dog-leg into the northwest lane, then turn down again for the run-in to 'wheel-over'. *Shoysa* was the longest ship he had ever had to anchor in such restricted conditions. He moved out to the starboard wing, avoided the grotesquely twisted corpses, took a visual bearing of Jugra Hill ... and then the sentry was speaking. He was pointing across the starboard bow — two huge planes were lumbering across the horizon, a red star on their tails.

Russians: Hok could recognize them anywhere, from his reserve training. He watched the sleek bombers shrieking silently across the bow; they opened out, then flew down the port side ... and, there, he spotted the outlines of the patrol boats, the UN Straits' Patrol Force which had been shadowing them for so long. They were much nearer, closing in, less than three miles and just abaft the beam.

Tumelaka sighted them at the same moment: it was 1740 — only twenty minutes until they reached the entrance of the separation zone.

'They're closing in, Tumelaka...' Hok shouted.

The terrorist leader looked up, then darted to the ship's broadcast. 'Activate all charges,' he commanded, shouting into the mic. 'Are the prisoners locked in the engine room yet?'

There was a long pause and then the voice of the second-in-command was on the line: 'Scuttling parties are on their way, sir. Charges being activated as ordered. All prisoners secured below.'

Hok jumped back into the wheelhouse.

Tumelaka dashed to the radio telephone. 'This is *Shoysa Maru*... Call off your boats. No one, repeat, no one, is to come further north. D'ye hear, no boat is to come any closer ... and order your bombers to stay out.' Tumelaka was quivering with rage. Hok turned away: *Shoysa* must not be sunk now — she was so nearly through...

Less than a minute later, Port Dickson Radio was warning all shipping at the northern entrance to heave-to. Hok strolled to the centre of the bridge, alone with his thoughts.

What could Tim and Hamzah do now? At this stage, any attempt at destroying Tumelaka would be suicidal, for the ship and the Straits were in his power. And as Johnny glanced again at the time, 1745 already, he noted the first change in bearing of the nearest smudge off to port.

'They're turning back,' he yelled. 'They're leaving you alone, Tumelaka.'

Tumelaka did not answer. He was watching his demolition parties dropping through the tank hatches along the upper deck: apart from the first two forward tanks, they seemed to have selected each alternate main cargo tank, along the midship-line — and also the engine room, presumably, out of sight below. He counted seven tanks in all. Hok returned to his chart table and checked his anchor bearings for the last time. In twenty minutes, he'd alter to starboard 340° — and he would reduce speed, whatever Tumelaka ordered. Johnny was on time for his ETA at the separation zone, and in the failing light he should find his bearings. He would be eight miles from 'let go' at 1800: forty minutes steaming. But anything could happen during the approach. He glanced at Tim Simkins, on his feet now, his face tense in the shadows, waiting...

Five minutes passed in silence, Tumelaka scanning the horizon through his binoculars. The patrol boats had disappeared. The sky was empty.

'Ready, pilot?'

'Ready. I alter up in five minutes.'

Tumelaka picked up the mic. 'All section parties muster at boarding stations,' he commanded, calmer now. 'Boats are not to be manned until ordered.' He beckoned to his signalman. 'Call up the FACs,' he snapped. 'Tell 'em to close the ship and lie off.'

Johnny Hok was at the radar: Jugra Hill and One Fathom Bank were spot-on. 'Time to alter course,' he said. 'Starboard fifteen, helmsman. Steer 340°.'

Hok sighed: he had piloted *Shoysa* to the crucial point, at least. Six o'clock and the alteration to the northward already started: forty minutes and it would be all over, one way or the other.

He was five minutes early, but he could switch on navigation lights, in case he forgot: he found the switches, walked out to check. Green and red burning brightly... How often he had gone through the same ritual — but even during this nightmare, ships had to navigate safely, obey the rules. The steaming light above them glowed, and on the fo'c'sle head the for'd steaming light shone from the stump mast between the winches.

Then he saw them, five smudges, broad on the port bow, pinpoints of white at their centres.

'Course 340°, master.'

Johnny crouched over the pelorus: the Japanese helmsman had understood. And those white blotches had grown into bow waves: above those creaming Vs, the gun shields and the bridges of fast attack craft were easily recognizable now.

Hamzah was right: Tumelaka had, from the beginning, intended to sink the ship.

A faint light showed forward of the port beam, and Johnny peered at it through his glasses. A flashing white, every five seconds — it didn't add up. And as he searched again he saw two quick flashing green lights, winking already in the twilight, just for'd of the beam. They could be temporary wreck markers after this morning's collision.

Johnny longed desperately to stop, to let up for a few minutes. His gamble, by playing arrogantly with the hijackers, had paid off — but for how much longer now? It was already twenty past six.

'I'm coming on to my anchoring course,' Johnny shouted from the starboard wing. '"Let go" in twenty minutes.' He called to the helmsman: 'Port fifteen. Steer 285°.'

He hastened inside, knocked her revs back to twelve knots. The chief engineer was nattering at the back, watching the television which was monitoring the poor wretches locked in the engine room.

Hok was past caring for his own skin. 'Tumelaka, you bastard, are you going to drown them — just like that?'

An evil smirk spread across Tumelaka's shining face. 'Yes, Mister Pilot, I am.' He pulled out his pistol. 'And now, get on with your job. You're too bloody slow.'

'I'm waiting for her to drop back… Takes time in this ship. The helmsman is dead on course.'

'How long before you drop the anchor?'

'"Let go" in sixteen minutes. There's no one on the fo'c'sle head. She won't anchor herself.' He pushed the telegraph to 'slow'.

Tumelaka was strapping on his bandolier, checking his pistol. 'I'm going for'd,' he said, 'and taking my rearguard with me. I'll pass my orders through the fo'c'sle phone.' He nodded at Hamzah, who had silently moved up behind them. 'Cover me, Hamzah,' he snapped. 'Bring that Englishman. He'll be anchoring the ship.'

'I'll flash my lamp twice for "let go",' Hok shouted. 'You'd better take this torch too, in case communications fail.'

Hok heard the snap as Hamzah slid off the safety catch of his automatic. Tim was dragged towards the door at the back of the bridge and pushed through it. Johnny could still hear Tumelaka's laughter while they waited outside for the lift.

Twilight was ending. Darkness was shutting in, and in the gloom five dark silhouettes were creeping close to the port side, at less than a cable. Johnny was crouching again across the bearing ring: six degrees to go. He hoped Tim would reach the Blake slip in time, because *Shoysa* would be into her final turn in six minutes.

He could see the dark figures scuttling beneath the deck lighting. Tumelaka was leading, Tim next, then the signalman, and then the Malay guard, bringing up the rear.

The bearing of One Fathom Bank was 'on'.

'Port twenty, helmsman.' Hok smiled at the exhausted man. 'Big turn this time — to 122°.'

He gesticulated that they were into the final turn, to stem the tide. The man showed his white teeth, shook his head, fixed his eyes on the heading ticking in the compass tape above him.

Hok moved the engine controls back to stop. He'd give her a minute, then go astern. He could just see the confused water on Amazon Maru Shoal. It looked close, and *Shoysa*'s counter would not clear it by much.

The fo'c'sle phone was buzzing.

'Pins out,' Simkins's voice said. 'Anchor ready for letting go.'

'You alone?'

'No.'

'Stand by, then…'

Johnny Hok suddenly felt very alone. With only a silent Japanese seaman by his side and a half-witted chief engineer at the rear, the bridge of this gigantic ship was a lonely place.

There was one consolation only: whilst Tumelaka and his devils were on board, all those left in *Shoysa Maru* still had a few moments to live.

CHAPTER TWENTY-FIVE

Tim felt the way coming off the ship as, standing by the enormous Blake slip, hammer in hand, he peered aft to the dim lights showing in *Shoysa*'s wheelhouse, 1300 feet away. And in that wheelhouse, the fate of the ship (and possibly the existence of the Malacca Strait waterway) lay in the hands of the imperturbable Johnny Hok. The ship was heeling to her final turn — and he saw the bridge structure leaning against the night horizon.

The pin was out, and he had taken off the brake. From between the massive winches, one eye on the bridge, the phone to his ear, he tried to watch what was going on twenty metres away...

Tumelaka's FACs were obviously alongside, ninety feet below, for most of the assault troops had already scrambled over the rail; the ends of the jumping ladders, which had remained rigged, had trailed in the water since the hijack began. He could see Tumelaka leaning over the rail and shouting at the laggards. He had turned on his radio-man, and was cursing him to get cracking over the side. He yelled at Jaafar, who ran aft to the furthest ladder. 'My God,' Tim muttered, 'he's too far away now...'

Jaafar flipped the first ladder hooks over the rail and let the ladder fall. Another of his men was slipping the next ladder; Jaafar skipped him, rushed to Number Three — only Number Two remained — and then Tim saw the first of the FACs disappearing into the darkness. The ship was shuddering as she went astern.

'Stand by, Tim...' Hok's voice was very faint.

'*Stand by.*'

Tim watched the horizon sliding across the bow and saw a bird swirling through the glare of the steaming light. The ship must be halfway through her turn to stem the tide. Thank God, someone had sensibly stopped the east-bound traffic, for *Shoysa* must be broadside across the channel — and then suddenly he sensed that something was wrong. The swing had slowed, and a tremor was rippling the plating beneath his feet.

'Tim,' Hok was shouting down the phone, 'we're aground aft...'

Tim saw the white crests of confused seas frothing off the starboard quarter where it was very dark...

'*Let go!*' A light flashed twice from the bridge windows. He knocked off the ship, jumped clear.

The gigantic shackles nudged forwards, then hustled along the deck to the lip of the hawse pipe, dust flying into the weird light.

Tim heard the splash. The Japanese shackle markings were indecipherable — but the cable was slowing now — thirty-five metres, Johnny had asked for. He ran to the winch and when the cable had stopped running, he wound on the brake.

'Brake's on,' he yelled up the phone. 'Don't know how much cable's out, Johnny — about ten shackles...' He ran to the side, watched the cable tautening as the bows began swinging back, when the tide caught her. 'She's right across the channel,' he whispered to himself in the loneliness of the fo'c'sle. *Shoysa* was hard aground aft, and the tide was forcing the bows against the cable.

'How's the cable grow?' It was Hok again, yelling down the phone.

'Port beam, bar-taut.'

Tim heard a shout. At the rail stood Tumelaka, his automatic jumping as he sprayed the bridge. The tracer was floating upwards and Tim heard the crash of shattering glass. Tumelaka swung on his heel and Tim flung himself behind the winch as bullets flattened themselves in the steelwork behind him.

Jaafar Hamzah was shouting: 'Simkins...'

Bent double, Tim ran aft to the two remaining silhouettes at the rail. Tumelaka, his hands above his head, was stumbling athwartships, the barrel of Jaafar's gun jabbing viciously into the small of his back.

'Grab his pistol,' Jaafar shouted. 'On the deck, by the rail.'

Tim slithered to the ship's side and picked up the gleaming weapon. He ran back to Jaafar, who was forcing the pirate against the main oil lines.

'Guard him, Simkins.' Jaafar was loosening one of his grenades.

'*No*, Jaafar — Cherry's in the last boat.'

Hamzah slithered to a halt, turned briefly, then ran to the rail. He yelled in Indonesian down to the boat ninety feet below. He unhitched the grapnels and pushed the top rungs of the ladder outwards. Tim heard a cry in the night and then the roar of engines opening up.

Jaafar was running towards him, waving his gun. 'They've shoved off,' he shouted. 'I've got the bastard.' He grabbed Tumelaka by the scruff of the neck.

'I'm going down,' Tim snapped. 'Starting with the for'd tanks. I'll follow the electric cable.'

Jaafar jabbed again at the dazed pirate. 'I'm taking him to the bridge. For God's sake, hurry, Simkins. You could save this end of the ship.'

He shouted over his shoulder as he began running aft with his stumbling prisoner. 'They're timed for 1915. For God's sake, watch out for yourself.'

Tim fumbled for the torch which Hok had thrown him. He ran to the for'd tank. As he flung back the hatch, he yelled aft towards the bridge: 'Jaafar — *the engine room.*'

CHAPTER TWENTY-SIX

Tim whipped back the circular hatch. It was 1854 by his watch as he clambered through, down into the inky blackness. His feet slithered on the greasy rungs as he swung off into the black hole.

Ninety feet to the tank bottom and soon the weird light from the fo'c'sle head was a dim pinpoint far above his head. As he clambered downwards he forced himself to think clearly, to smother the panic mounting inside him.

These two for'd tanks, A and B, each had a capacity of 9,000 cubic metres, smaller than the others to reduce collision risks. He must time himself accurately: if he could, he would try to immunize G as well, the foremost midship lateral tank, one of the five largest in the ship — and then the stale stench of oil and damp were assailing him. He must be near the bottom soon. He was breaking every regulation in the book: *one spark only...* He prayed as he switched on his torch, which he had stupidly forgotten to do in his haste down the ladder...

Soon he was squelching through the sludge on the tank bottom. The electric cable gleamed in the torch beam, and he followed it to where it terminated in the centre of the tank.

The leads were connected by push-pull sockets to two connections on the top of a circular object, like a curling stone — it could have been an oyster-type mine, adapted for demolition work. The tension was making him clumsy as the seconds ticked away. Tim pulled off one of the leads, then saw the box close alongside, a timing device, its clock hands set to 1915. He traced the cable and carefully slipped off the two terminals. He picked up the box of tricks, slithered through the slime and carefully deposited it in the far corner of the tank. He sloshed back to the bottom of the ladder and began climbing frenziedly, hand-over-hand, feet slipping on the rungs beneath.

He had to stop three-quarters of the way up, gasping for air. Then at last, he was hauling himself over the lip — seven minutes, only seven minutes for one tank... It was already 1901.

Tim climbed across the transverse interconnecting lines, reached B hatch, flung it back on its hinges. He felt claustrophobic in the darkness. It was showing 1904 as he began slipping downwards.

His heart was pounding as, reckless now, he slithered down the greasy ladder, his world bounded by the light thrown by the torch. He felt the jerk, the shivering of the hull as the cable snatched to its anchor — and all about him in this stinking vault, the echoes boomed in the void, reverberating against his eardrums until he felt they would burst.

He was, Hok realized, only about one cable too far north of his DR. But as the stern struck, he was also aware that the error could be catastrophic. *Shoysa Maru*'s bows had swung back on the tide, held bar-taut by the anchor cable. Her heading was 170° and she lay, all 1350 feet of her, squarely across the northwest channel — and if the scuttling charges blew now...? He tried to raise Simkins on the fo'c'sle phone.

'Veer the cable on the brake. Quick, Tim...' For answer, there was only the soughing of the breeze. As he peered for'd to the flickering lights, he could see the cause of the unmanned phone — and he flung himself to the deck as the windows shattered to his left while bullets thudded into the back of the wheelhouse.

Hok dared not leave the bridge to take off the brake himself; he could not send the helmsman: he could never understand. He rushed to the radar, took his bearings, and slapped them on the chart: right in the centre of the northwest lane, bang in the middle, between Amazon Maru Shoal and the wreck in fifteen metres…

He tried the fo'c'sle phone again, shouted down the intercom. As he squinted forward, he could see a tiny figure disappearing into a tank hatch, way-up for'd. All the ladders had gone from the rail and the last of the terrorist's FACs was shoving off into the darkness. Two figures were half-running, half-stumbling aft along the deck towards the accommodation island. He ran to the radiotelephone.

'PAN … PAN … PAN…' He tried to keep his voice steady. 'This is *Shoysa Maru, Shoysa Maru, Shoysa Maru* —'

'Pass your message, *Shoysa.*'

'Aground in position 165° One Fathom Bank 3.5 miles. Tell all ships to keep clear. *Shoysa* may sink at any moment… Out.' He would amplify his signal when he could. He yelled at the Japanese chief engineer, who was cowering in the corner at the back of the bridge, his mind gone.

The door burst open as Tumelaka stumbled inwards, his hands crossed behind his head, and gasping for breath. Behind him was the Malay sergeant, his gun stabbing viciously into the terrorist's kidneys.

'The phone…' Hamzah grabbed the instrument and forced it into Tumelaka's grasp.

'Now talk: first in English…'

He stood back, pointed the gun at Tumelaka's chest. 'Speak.' Johnny Hok watched, mesmerized by the drama, as the minutes ticked by on the clock above them: 1902. Tumelaka, his eyes riveted to the second hand circling remorselessly, gasped into the radiotelephone: 'This is Tumelaka speaking, Tumelaka... Do you hear me, Lieutenant Kyai, Lieutenant Kyai, do you read me?'

It seemed like an eternity before communication was established on 2182 — and then, safety-catch off, Hamzah's barrel spiralling in front of him, Tumelaka began bartering for his life.

'Kyai,' he was speaking slowly and clearly. 'Close boat Number 1 immediately: you are to take off the prisoner, Miss Hok, and proceed at full speed with her to the Aruah islands, one mile to the east of Jemur light-structure. You are to wait until I join you in one of the Straits' patrol boats.' He hesitated, mesmerized by the gun barrel.

'Go on...' Hamzah hissed.

'The prisoner Hok is not, repeat, not, to be molested or harmed,' he ordered. 'The safety of your boat and your crew depend on the exchange of the unharmed woman with myself. She is not, repeat, not, to be molested or harmed. Do you understand?' His voice was unsteady. 'Wait until I join you. Repeat back your orders... This is Tumelaka, your commander... Over.'

The clock was showing 1906 as Kyai began reciting his orders in clipped English. Hamzah shoved the gun into Johnny's hands.

'Guard him, pilot,' he said brusquely. He was running to the door. 'Call up a Straits' patrol boat.'

'Where the hell are you going?' Johnny Hok shouted.

'The engine room,' Jaafar yelled over his shoulder. 'In eight minutes, it will blow itself to pieces.'

At the same minute, Timothy Simkins made his decision: alone in the forepart of the ship, with A and B tanks safe, he began slithering down the ladder into the enormous C tank, which was large enough to contain the entire cargo of one of yesterday's tankers. He tried to obliterate his imagination, curb his panic as he slithered down for the third time into the evil-smelling darkness. And he prayed to his God as never before: what if the charge exploded prematurely ... if he fell, injured ... if the after tanks went up, before he was out again? And how much time had he?

Again Tim was in the slime, striding towards the centre — the same drill, but longer this time, in this huge cavern. At last, the charge was harmless. He threshed back to the foot of the ladder and began his long haul upwards, the booming of the anchor cable as it snatched, aggravating his terror.

He was about halfway up, the sound of the snatching cable terrifying in this cavernous void, when he sighted the faint pinpoint of light, slowly growing larger. Without warning, he was suddenly flung backwards by a rippling shock. He was still hanging firmly by one hand, but the hammer blows which followed in rapid succession whipped his feet from the slippery rungs. Then there was another most violent explosion farther away, which jolted him back to the ladder. He heaved himself upwards, rung after rung, rung after rung...

Then he tasted the sweet air; he scrambled through the hatch and fell over the lip. Another shock shivered the ship as he stumbled aft along the deck, which was already down by the stem.

There was another distant explosion directly below him, jarring his backbone. Tim rushed aft, slithering to the accommodation island, and pushed open the screen door. The lift flat was in darkness, the power gone. He dashed outside again for the ladders. A trail of terrified Japanese men were struggling upwards from the engine room, blocking the route. Tim crossed to the port side and took the other ladders.

He burst through the wheelhouse door. Johnny Hok was there, speaking into the telephone. Jaafar, gun in hand, was watching Tumelaka, his eyes fixed on the pirate's face.

'D'you read, *Hammarskjöld*? We're sinking aft,' the pilot was coolly informing the UN Straits' patrol boat, 'but I reckon the upper deck will still be above water. You'll be all right on our port side: slack water here. Be glad to see you again, Michael.'

'I've got you on radar,' Voon replied. 'I'll be with you in ten minutes. Is the prisoner ready?'

'Yes,' Hok said. 'He's dangerous. There'll be two for you to take off — the prisoner and his guard.'

'Three,' Tim chipped in firmly. 'I'm going too.'

The Straits' patrol boat, *Dag Hammarskjöld*, bore off her bows and swung to port and into the night. Her engines growled, increasing to a roar, and then she was bouncing on her chine and hurtling through the darkness. She swung to port to clear the stricken tanker's bows, then turned back to her course for the Aruah islands.

'Three quarters of an hour,' the captain shouted above the wind, 'and we'll be there.'

Alone with his thoughts, Tim held on to the bridge side and watched *Shoysa Maru* settling across the channel. It was dark, but her silhouette blotted out the horizon to the eastward. Her bows jutted upwards at an angle of twenty degrees, her bulk high above the sea. Buoyant in her forepart, flooded aft, she was now totally blocking the channel.

In three quarters of an hour, it would be all over … and Tim rehearsed again the drill for the exchange which Jaafar and he intended. The terrorists could not be trusted but, at least, the balance was tilted in Cherry's favour. Their leader was of much greater value to the enemy than she was.

And then he saw Jemur's light, flashing regularly every five seconds, dead ahead. Twenty minutes later, *Dag Hammarskjöld* eased her revs and her inflatable was swung out. She left the rocks well to starboard where the surf curled lazily, white in the darkness. Two minutes later they sighted the enemy, hull down and alone, wallowing in the swell.

Jaafar held Tumelaka on the after deck while the two captains talked on the R/T — and then Tim saw the tiny smudge bobbing in the sea. A white bow-wave frothed and then the rubber boat was dancing towards them … and as he watched, he heard behind him the whine of *Dag Hammarskjöld*'s gun training on its mounting. The enemy's inflatable had stopped, lying off.

The R/T crackled again. The dinghy came on, drew alongside: two of its occupants were on either side of the little figure crouching between them, and then the patrol boat's sailors were taking the lines.

They gently handed her up the ladder. She stood on the deck for a second, swaying before him, a tiny figure in the darkness.

'You all right, Cherry?'

'Yes … oh, Tim…'

And then she was in his arms, sobbing against his chest.

Tim heard the splutter of the outboard. *Hammarskjöld*'s inflatable, the exchange prisoner, Tumelaka, lying on its bottom slats, opened up its outboard and threshed into the night.

The light from Jemur flickered regularly above the patrol boat. The beam swept across the water, the surface glistening where it touched; and in its gleam, the silhouettes of two launches showed briefly. They were moving fast, on opposite courses. In seconds they had vanished, swallowed by the night.

EPILOGUE

by Cheah Ho Yong

It is hoped that the drama of *Shoysa Maru* might still shake the world from its lethargy. The fact that a bunch of fanatics could hold the most powerful naval superpowers to ransom has left the politicians and the shipping world reeling. The hijacking of an ULCC, once only a bad dream, had, in a few hours, become reality … and, after the *Shoysa Maru* affair, the nightmare can never be fully dispelled.

The inquiry was a formal business, wrapped up efficiently and impersonally: no one, specifically, was to blame for the closing of the Straits. For deep-draught ships, the Pacific Ocean was severed from the Indian Ocean for several weeks. And if it had not been for a man of Simkins's calibre, the results could have been even more catastrophic. Though this has cost the maritime nations billions, because of the enforced haul through Lombok, it is gratifying that Simkins was honoured by the Japanese government for his part in the incident.

The forepart of *Shoysa Maru* did not sink. Though she lifted her anchor, she remained stuck, sunk by her flooded engine rooms, pumping compartment and her four lateral cargo tanks. She was pivoted by her stern to the seabed, on the edge of the Amazon Maru Shoal. The tugs succeeded in dragging her bows round and eventually cleared the northwest lane.

One thing, now that the song and dance is over, rings out loudly and clearly: the chaotic and diverse navigational systems adorning the world's vital arteries provided the climate in which the hijackers succeeded.

Without swift agreement (and that demands compromise, from all nations) upon international standard traffic procedures, similar to those observed by air traffic, the planet is doomed to a creeping death from the oceans.

— Cheah Ho Yong Head of Investigation Division, Central Narcotics Bureau

A NOTE TO THE READER

Dear Reader,

If you have enjoyed the novel enough to leave a review on **Amazon** and **Goodreads**, then we would be truly grateful.

Sapere Books is an exciting new publisher of brilliant fiction and popular history.

To find out more about our latest releases and our monthly bargain books visit our website:
saperebooks.com